×4D
×

DISCARDED
BAKER CO. PUBLIC LIBRARY

VS Western MAR 2 4 1995
Hogan, Ray
The man from Barranca Negra

25¢ fine charged
for cards missing
from b

Baker County Public Library
2400 Resort St,
Baker City, OR 97814

DEMCO

The Man from Barranca Negra

Ray Hogan

was born in Willow Springs, Missouri, where his father was a town marshal. When he was five, the Hogan family moved to Albuquerque where Ray still lives in the foothills of the Sandia and Manzano mountains. It was while listening to his father and other old-timers tell tales from the past that Ray was inspired to recast these tales in fiction. What is most impressive about Hogan's Western novels is the consistent quality with which each is crafted, the compelling depth of his characters, and his ability to juxtapose the complexities of human conflict into narratives always as intensely interesting as they are emotionally involving.

THE MAN FROM BARRANCA NEGRA

Ray Hogan

ROUNDUP LARGE PRINT
HAMPTON, NEW HAMPSHIRE

Library of Congress Cataloging-in-Publication Data

Hogan, Ray, 1908–
    The man from Barranca Negra / Ray Hogan.
      p.   cm.
    ISBN 0-7927-2013-X
    ISBN 0-7927-2012-1 (pbk.)
[PS3558.O3473M26   1994]   93-48209
813′.54—dc20   CIP

Copyright © 1964, by Ace Books, Inc.

All Rights Reserved

Published in Large Print by arrangement with Donald MacCampbell, Inc. by Chivers North America
1 Lafayette Road, Hampton, NH 03842—0015

Printed in Great Britain

CHAPTER ONE

With the furious storm raging about him, Ben Jordan halted. He was high in the towering Mogollon Mountains of New Mexico Territory, struggling to follow a trail that cut a precarious course along a rocky ridge. He probed the wet, half darkness with anxious eyes. Although it was only mid-afternoon, it seemed night was almost upon him.

He was soaked to the skin, despite his slicker, and chilled to the bone from the snow-tinged rain. Water cascaded from him and the weary buckskin he rode in a hundred small rivulets. The trail had become a sea of flowing mud, the entire mountainside a sheet of glistening water. Arroyos were running full, and had become wild, turbulent rivers of boiling, brown slush that swept everything before them.

Lightning flashed vividly, now and then striking one of the towering pines that studded the slope, creating an eerie glow and setting up a hissing and crackling that blended with the continual grumble of thunder.

Jordan had no idea of how far he was from a settlement, or even if there was such in the area. And it had been hours since he had noted a miner's cabin or squatter's shack. But the trail he followed appeared to be a main course; it would lead eventually to somewhere. At this point, however, it made little difference; he wanted only to get in out of the hammering rain to dry and warm himself.

It was days since he had ridden out of Mexico and the comfort of the hot Sonora sun. Now, wet and cold, he was having vague regrets, wishing that he had not accepted Tom Ashburn's offer and that he had not given up the ranch in the *Barranca Negra*, since that morning when Mexican bandits swooped down, attacked, and killed his father and stepmother.

Perhaps he should have stayed put on the ranch deep in the black-walled gorge; maybe he should have toughed it out, continued the never ending war with the renegades that had begun the day his father, Dave Jordan, and he, then only a small boy, had settled in the *Barranca Negra*. Matters had improved somewhat a few years later when the elder Jordan had met and married a Mexican woman; the *gringo patron* and his son became more acceptable to the natives at that point.

But in the end it mattered little. The bandits' bullets recognized no distinction, and the letter from Dave Jordan's old friend, Tom Ashburn, arriving two months later, was most opportune. It offered him the job as foreman on his vast Lazy A spread in north-eastern New Mexico. Ben had lost no time accepting. He gave away what was left of the ranch in the *Barranca Negra*, packed what few possessions he owned in his saddlebags, and rode out.

In his heart he knew it was the right thing to do. Although he had come to love the country he grew up in, there was nothing there for him; the ranch was a poor, starve-out affair at best. Ben Jordan knew that, admitted it, but change always comes hard to any man.

Sitting there, high on the storm-swept mountain, wet and cold, he told himself again that he had made the right decision and by such he would abide despite the bitter welcome being extended him by the elements.

He stared ahead. He could see no sign of shelter through the whipping gusts. All that was visible were the swaying, tortured pines shifting under the storm's impact, the wetly shining rocks, the deeply grooved trail that was now an onrushing stream.

Lightning glared beyond the ridge to his left, and was followed instantly by a clap of thunder. The buckskin trembled beneath him. At once the rain seemed to increase and somewhere behind him came a new roaring as an arroyo, filled to capacity, broke free of its bounds and began to pour down the slope in a new channel.

Jordan urged his pony on. The footing was slippery, dangerous and the horse moved reluctantly. If there was no hope of reaching a settlement, then he must soon find shelter of some sort for the buckskin and himself. They were both about finished. A low butte facing away from the slanting rain would afford some protection. He was avoiding the thick stands of trees, prime targets, it would seem, for the jagged streaks of lightning.

A hundred yards farther along Jordan again pulled to a halt and dismounted. It was too much for the buckskin to carry a rider and maintain his footing in the swirling mud and water. Walking out ahead of the worn horse, Jordan pressed on, able to follow the trail now only because of the lack of brush and rock in its course.

A half hour later Jordan saw ahead a lower crest, actually the summit of a saddle looping between two peaks. There the trail dropped off the high ridge along which he was traveling, and appeared through the murk to angle off the rim and slice diagonally across a broad swale and enter the forest. He did not like the idea of going into the trees but the hollow itself was low and considerably sheltered from the full force of the howling storm.

Hopeful of finding at last the protection he sought, he pushed on, keeping well back from the edge of the ridge which here dropped off steeply into the dark depths of a canyon. Although the footing was uncertain, the ground was fairly level, and he moved on, leading the buckskin at a good pace.

And then, suddenly the world was nothing more than a vacuum of blinding, blue light filled with tremendous sound. He felt the buckskin wrench the reins from his hand, heard him neigh in terror. Jordan was aware of a powerful force striking him, slamming him flat into the swirling water and mud.

Half blinded, he struggled to his feet. A peculiar prickling sensation filled his body and he was slightly stunned. He looked about. Lightning had struck a tree no more than fifty feet away, and had split it down the center, smoking and sizzling in the pouring rain.

There was no sign of the buckskin. Jordan wheeled, hurried to the rim of the canyon. He waited for the next spread of light. It came at once. He saw the luckless horse far below, wedged between two massive boulders. There was no doubt that the fall, when he had shied and gone over the edge, had killed him instantly.

Ben Jordan stood quietly on the brink of the chasm for several minutes while a sense of loss possessed him. The buckskin had been a good horse, a faithful companion. But there was nothing he could do for him now.

And he was, himself, afoot, with all his gear lost, with no hope of replacement until he reached civilization.

He moved on, following the trail across the long swale, still heading for the trees lying on its far side. The rain continued its onslaught, freighted with frequent and vivid flashes of lightning and rolling, crackling thunder. When he reached the lowest point of the hollow, a twenty foot wide arroyo blocked his route.

He hesitated momentarily, then ventured into the knee deep torrent cautiously. The current was strong, tugged at him relentlessly. Legs spread to steady himself, he made his way slowly. He reached the center, braced himself for the final effort—and then, suddenly, he was going over.

Something moving beneath the surface of the boiling water, a small log perhaps, or a bush ripped free of its moorings, had caught at his feet and tripped him. The force of the arroyo spun him about and thrust him backward. He fought to remain upright, failed, and went down into the churning, roily water. Choking, gasping, he managed to roll over, striving frantically to get his feet under him again as he bobbed erratically in the rushing current.

He touched ground, and steadied himself. Bucking the arroyo's force, he managed to pull himself upright again, and stagger his way to the edge of the wash. He dragged himself out of the surging flood, and halted, sucking deep for breath. His clothing was plastered to him, and seemed to weigh a hundred pounds and his feet were awash inside his boots. He sat down, emptied them, and noticed at that instant that he had lost his gun.

He rose, turned up the slope, dismissing the loss with no further thought; recovering the weapon would have been impossible. Worn to exhaustion, he trudged on. He must stop now. He was physically incapable of going any farther. A bush, a low tree, a ledge of rock, anything would serve as shelter.

A sudden flare of light shattered the darkness, and illuminated the entire slope. Hope surged through him. In the brief break he thought he had seen the outlines of a cabin. He waited for the next flash, eyes straining into the gloom. A jagged finger ripped the murk once more.

A long sigh escaped his lips. It was a cabin—shelter at last! Even if uninhabited it would provide protection from the storm, a place to rest, to remove and dry his clothing and wait out the storm.

He struggled up the grade, slipping, falling, hurrying desperately to reach the structure. As he drew nearer he saw that it was a crude, log affair, that it appeared to be in fair condition. Beyond it a short distance stood a second building, a shed of some sort. His spirits lifted higher. Someone likely was there; a miner possibly. There would be food, a fire, dry clothing.

He stumbled up the last of the incline, reached the level upon which the cabin had been built. He lurched toward the doorway, now seeing faint light seeping through a shuttered window. His hand grasped the wooden latch, and lifted it.

The door opened and he half fell as he entered. His head came up swiftly and his pulse quickened as he stared into the muzzle of a pistol.

CHAPTER TWO

'Don't ... move...'

The command came from a man hunched in an opposite corner. The words were halting, labored.

Jordan froze. A lantern placed near the crouched figure spread a small circle of light before him. Ben looked sharply at the man. His brush jacket had been thrown back. The entire right side of his chest was blood soaked. There was another wound in his leg. The pistol in his hand wavered uncertainly.

Ben closed the door with his heel, started

to rise. 'Here, better let me—'

The hunched shape stiffened. 'Don't try—' he began and lapsed into silence. After a moment he motioned with his weapon. 'Get in the light. Got to see if—'

Jordan advanced slowly, stopped within the lantern's yellow glow. 'You're in a bad way,' he said. 'Let me help.'

The man stared at Ben with hot, glittering eyes. He was a thin-faced, dark individual. 'You're—you're not one of them,' he said finally, and let his arm fall as though the pistol's weight was more than he could manage. 'Who are you?'

'Name's Jordan. Up from Mexico,' Ben said, dropping to his knees beside the man. 'What happened to you?'

There was a long minute as though the man were having difficulty concentrating. Then, 'Outlaws. Jumped me late yesterday afternoon. Gave them the slip but caught a couple of bullets... Thought—thought you were one of them.'

Jordan examined the man's breast. It was a bad wound, one that left nothing to be done. Death could be only a matter of hours.

'Not me,' Ben said, pulling the jacket into place. 'Got trapped in the storm. Lost my horse over a cliff when lightning hit close by. Was looking for shelter when I saw your cabin.'

'Don't belong to me,' the wounded man

said. 'Like you—come across it after I got hit—and was looking for a place to hole up. Name's Woodward—Walt Woodward.'

Jordan reached for the man's hand, shook it gently. He glanced about the cabin. It was bare, and apparently had not been lived in for some time. Several insistent leaks drip-dropped from the ceiling and the glass in a window high on the rear wall had been broken out.

'Little heat would feel good,' Ben said, his eyes pausing on the fireplace and a scatter of split wood and pine knots near it. 'I'll get a fire going, then we'll see what we can do about those wounds of yours.'

Woodward smiled weakly. 'Be a waste of time,' he said. 'Been around, seen how these things go.'

Jordan was busy at his chore. 'We'll give it a try, anyway. Never can tell.'

But he knew there was little point to it. Not even the expert attention of a physician could help Walt Woodward now. Not only had he lost far too much blood, but the bullet in his chest had damaged his lung.

When the fire was going well Jordan turned, began to prowl the cabin. He located a gunnysack, stuffed it into the gaping window, closed out the driving rain. The storm still raged, slamming against the cabin in fitful gusts and blasts.

The flames in the fireplace mounted, filled

the room with warmth and light. Jordan knelt beside Woodward again. The man was propped in the corner, his back resting against a pair of saddlebags. Ben pointed to them.

'Any grub in there? Coffee?'

Woodward shook his head. 'No. No food. Could sure use a drink of water. You got any?'

Jordan said, 'No. Lost everything when my horse bolted. But I can fix you up.'

He found a tin can left by some previous tenant. Holding it beneath one of the steady drips, he rinsed out the dust, then allowed it to fill. He handed it to Woodward.

'May taste a bit rusty...'

Woodward seized the can, drank greedily. When he had finished he set the container on the floor beside him. He studied Jordan with bright, feverish eyes.

'From Mexico, eh? You a 'breed? Don't look like a Mexican.'

Ben, faintly angered, said, 'No, I'm neither, not that it makes any difference. Just happens I grew up down there.'

'Headed for where?'

'North-eastern part of the territory. Going to work for Tom Ashburn, the Lazy A ranch.'

Except for the suffering Woodward, it was pleasant in the cabin, out of the shrieking storm. The room had warmed, and was now filled with the soft glow of the fire. Ben took up the can, and filled it again with water and then set it near the flames to heat.

'Get some hot water, I'll see what I can do for—'

'Forget it,' Woodward said. 'Just not in the cards for me.'

Jordan stared into the dancing flames. 'You mentioned outlaws; what happened? They try to hold you up?'

Woodward shifted his position, slowly, painfully. 'Fire feels good,' he murmured. Then, 'Yeh, four of them, four men. Tried to rob me. Made a run for it. Got away except—except maybe I didn't really get away after all.'

Jordan was silent, wondering why outlaws would attempt to halt Woodward unless the man were carrying something of value. He did not appear to be a man of wealth. And if there were other reasons—

'You're—you're wondering why,' the wounded man said, reading Jordan's thoughts. Lightning crashed somewhere back up the slope, briefly filling the room with a lurid white light. Woodward waited until the roll of thunder died. 'I'll tell you why, Jordan. Money—cash money. Quite a lot of it. That's what they wanted.'

Ben glanced up in surprise. 'Why tell me? Aren't you afraid I'll—'

'Afraid you'll take it from me, that what

you're trying to say? Maybe, but I don't think so. You're not the kind to rob a dying man of all he's got—not when he has a wife at home waiting for him to show up.'

Woodward paused, out of breath. He managed a half smile. 'The truth, Jordan—was on my way home—carrying the money I got from selling a ranch of mine—down Arizona way—every cent I have in the world—it's here in these saddlebags. Twenty—twenty thousand dollars.'

'Twenty thousand dollars!' Ben echoed softly.

'Figure you're a man I can trust,' Woodward said, his voice sinking lower. 'Want my wife to have that money. She needs it. Something to keep her rest of her life. No country for a woman alone—broke. There's a thousand in it for you if—if you'll see to it—'

Jordan frowned. 'I don't want any of it.'

Woodward forced a smile. 'Knew you'd say that. Reason I'm asking you. As a favor, Jordan—to a dying man. Will you see she gets it?'

Ben stared into the flames. 'I don't know,' he said slowly. 'Not sure I can, or want to. I've got a job to take over. Ought to be there now. And I've lost my horse.'

'Won't be out of your way none. And I give you my horse. He's in the shack behind the cabin. Maybe not in too good a shape—but he'll take you where you're going.'

Jordan considered. 'Where is your wife?'

'Town by the name of Langford—about a day's ride on the other side of the Lazy A outfit.'

'You know Ashburn?'

'No. Heard of the Lazy A, that's all.'

Woodward paused, coughed deeply and softly. Ben dipped a finger into the can of water. It was just beginning to warm.

'Be no problem,' Woodward continued. 'Just ride in. Ask somebody—anybody where Ollie—Olivia—Woodward lives. They'll show you. Give her the saddlebags and—that's it. Want you to keep a thousand for your trouble.'

Jordan said, 'No, but the horse will be a favor.'

'He's yours—along with the gear—good saddle—rifle—pistol, too. See yours is missing.'

'Lost it fording an arroyo.'

Woodward nodded, waited. 'You giving me your promise?'

Ben said, 'My word on it.'

Walt Woodward sank back gratefully. He wiped at his lips with the back of his hand. 'One bit of luck—' he murmured, 'having an honest man show up here. Could've been somebody who would've taken the money and rode on ... I'm obliged to you, Jordan.'

'Forget it,' Ben said. 'I appreciate the horse and gear. Losing mine was a blow.'

'Like to say one more thing—about the money. Don't trust anybody. Hand it over to my wife—nobody else. Like your promise on that, too...'

'You've got it.'

Woodward sighed heavily. His fingers tugged at the edge of his sheepskin brush jacket. 'Might as well have this, too. Won't do me any good—where I'm going. And you'll need it. Gets cold in these hills—at night.'

Jordan said, 'Thanks, again,' and let it drop.

Woodward pulled himself around, seeking more comfort. 'Want to warn you about those outlaws. Four men—got on my trail outside Tucson. Never shook them until yesterday.'

'How'd they find out you were carrying all that cash?'

'Who knows? Must have got tipped off by somebody—but it's what they're after—no other reason. Recognized them. Man named Bart Crawford's the leader. Big fellow—riding a black horse—and Cleve Aaron. He's one of them. He's on a bay. Arlie Davis is forking a bay, only it's a small horse—like an Indian pony. Fourth man will be on a gray. They call him Gates.'

'Sound like you know them pretty well.'

'Ought to—been up against them before. Real hard-cases, everyone of them. When you pull out of here, keep your eyes peeled. They'll still be looking for me.'

'I'll watch,' Jordan said.

The water in the can had begun to simmer. Picking up a small stick, Ben pushed it away from the fire. He glanced at Woodward.

'There any extra shirt or something in your saddlebags? Need to make a bandage.'

Woodward said, 'Never mind, Jordan. I'm feeling all right. Doctoring won't do me any good now—could use another drink.'

Ben started to empty the can. The wounded man said, 'Leave it—being warm, maybe—it'll melt some of the ice—in my belly.'

Jordan picked up the container. It was cool enough to hold. He passed it to Woodward who wrapped his hands about it.

'Feels good.' he murmured. After a moment he began to sip the tepid water. 'Little whiskey in this—sure would—help.'

Ben tossed the remainder of the wood on the fire. He was dry now, and beginning to grow drowsy. He yawned, stretched out full length before the flames. He glanced at Woodward.

'Sure there's nothing I can do for you?'

'Nothing,' Woodward replied. 'Reckon I'd—better let you get—some sleep.' He reached out his hand. 'Want to say it—again, Jordan. Obliged to you.'

Ben took the man's fingers into his own. They were cold despite the warm can he had been holding. 'It's all right. And don't worry. I'll see that your wife gets the money.'

'A—great relief,' Woodward, said, sighing. 'Good night—Jordan.'

CHAPTER THREE

Ben awoke cold and stiff. He lay quiet for a minute listening. The rain had finally stopped. It was still dark but he guessed the hour must be somewhere near dawn. The fire had gone out and a damp chill again possessed his body. He thought then of Walt Woodward and sat up quickly.

Woodward was hunched in his corner. He had pulled the saddlebags from behind his back, had them laid out across his legs along with the sheepskin jacket. The man's face was a sallow mask, his eyes deep, shadowy pockets.

Jordan rolled to his feet swiftly, and crossed to where Woodward sat. He reached out, shook the man's shoulder gently. Woodward aroused. His hand dropped to the pistol lying on the floor at his side. Then he relaxed.

'Jordan—' he muttered. 'Jordan—thought for—a second it...' the words trailed off.

Ben crouched nearer to the man. 'Woodward! Woodward! Listen to me. The storm's quit. We can get out of here. Is there a settlement around close? I'll try to get you to—'

'Don't—bother...' The man's voice was no more than a low croaking sound. 'Don't bother. Just get—the—money—to my—wife—you promised—me...'

Woodward's head sagged forward abruptly and he started to topple. Ben caught him, laid him back. He felt for a pulse, and found none. Walt Woodward was dead.

Jordan got to his feet. He stood for a time looking down at the man's tormented face, and then turned away. The cabin was cold. A fire would feel good but there was no wood left, and outside all would be soaked. He stared into the gray ashes of the fireplace, considering his next move.

It would be senseless to take Woodward's body on to Langford and his widow. With only one horse it would be a long, drawn out, near impossible task. And there was no point. Better to bury the man there and move on, and fulfill his promise to deliver the money to Ollie Woodward.

He wheeled to the door and went outside. The sky had cleared and the first rays of the sun were beginning to spray upward from the eastern horizon in flaring fingers of color. The air was cold and damp and water lay about in low places wherever he looked. But it would not long remain, he knew. Once the sun began to climb and send forth its sucking heat, the moisture would disappear.

He walked to the rear cabin and entered. Woodward's horse, a handsome sorrel gelding with white forelegs greeted him with an anxious whicker. Ben comforted the animal, then led him into the open and picketed him on a small patch of grass a few yards up the slope. The sorrel was a fine looking horse, much better than the buckskin.

Leaving the gelding to graze, Jordan hunted around until he found a broken spade and with that dug a shallow grave. He buried Woodward, covered the mound with rocks to keep away the wolves and coyotes. Then, wearing the dead man's jacket, and with the bulging saddlebags heavy with gold coins and packets of currency, he mounted the sorrel and rode down the mountain.

The trail was again visible, the rainwater having drained away, and he had no difficulty in following it except when he would come upon a gash cut at right angles to its course where an arroyo, surging downward from the high peaks, had slashed a channel.

He had no idea how far it was to the next settlement but, as before, figured the trail would eventually bring him out at some point. He was not particularly disturbed about it since a northerly course would take him in the right direction and lead him finally to the Lazy A ranch of Tom Ashburn.

Food was the pressing problem; he had not eaten since the previous morning and hunger was now a gnawing pain within him. Around noon he saw a long-eared jackrabbit. Using Walt Woodward's rifle, he killed it.

He halted then and roasted the animal over a low fire. The meat was tough and stringy, almost tasteless for lack of salt, but satisfied his stomach, and he rode on an hour later feeling better.

As the miles passed he appreciated more and more the qualities of the sorrel, and as well, the country surrounding him. Everywhere the land was green and beautiful, much different from the dry wastes of the *Barranca Negra*. He wondered if the country where Tom Ashburn had his ranch was like this, and found himself hoping it would be.

It should be no chore raising fine cattle in a land so lush. Grass covered the ground in a deep, green blanket anywhere a man looked. Water was plentiful. It was strange that he saw no ranches, no farms; then remembered that the area was devoted mainly to mining.

Men searching for gold or silver had no time for anything else.

He pressed on, the sorrel seemingly tireless. They topped out one succeeding rise after another and the realization gradually came to Ben Jordan that he would be forced to spend the night in the open again. But that was no problem. Being under a roof with Walt Woodward was the first time he had not slept on the trail in over a week. He glanced at the sky, thankful that no rain-heavy clouds hovered about. It would be cold, but not wet.

Again he had to think of food. He began to watch the brush and scrubby growth that fringed the deep forest, alert for another rabbit, preferably a cottontail or a young jack this time. Venison would taste good but he rebelled at the thought of wasting a whole deer for only one or two meals.

He killed another rabbit a short time later, a young jack, and halted there to skin and cook it. He would get the meal out of the way, he decided, and at the same time allow the gelding to rest. Then he would ride on until full darkness overtook him before he bedded down for the night.

He had just finished eating, and was stamping out the embers of his fire when he chanced to look back over his trail, rising and falling as it climbed in and out of the long swales and topped out the ridges lying in between.

At first, he saw nothing, only the deep, rich green of the land, and then suddenly riders came into his vision. Interest stirred through him and was followed quickly by alarm. They were at a considerable distance but were moving toward him at steady pace, coming along the exact path he had taken.

Of course they could be simply fellow pilgrims, headed in the same general direction; Walt Woodward's money was making him suspicious, jumpy. And then, as they moved out into the last of the bright sunlight and he had a good look at them, he knew his fears were warranted.

There were four men in the party.

CHAPTER FOUR

Ben Jordan swung to the saddle quickly and wheeled into the deep shadows off trail. He could not be certain they had seen him yet, but that they were following him, tracking him by the hoof prints left by the sorrel in the soft ground, there was no doubt.

He studied the men, striving to identify them and thus rule out all possibility of error. He waited until they crossed the next shallow valley, climbed the grade and were again outlined on the horizon. A big man on a black horse—that would be Crawford. Two on dark brown animals; a fourth on a gray. He was not wrong. They were the outlaws.

He moved off at once, putting the gelding to a lope. He had a good lead on the four men, and darkness was not far off. If he could reach rocky ground, a place where the sorrel would leave no prints, there was a good chance of losing Crawford and his bunch. But as the miles wore on that hope dwindled. The heavy rainfall had soaked the country generally, and there was no hard ground within reach.

He began to curve then toward the higher hills, aiming for the ridges and peaks. It would be rougher going with plenty of granite ledges and benches that would not mark his passage. He rode on, pushing the gelding, now beginning to labor as he moved upgrade. Daylight was disappearing slowly. Jordan, grim, looked ahead. Another mile, perhaps two, and he would be at the foot of the mountain. And by then it should be night.

He reached the first upthrusting of solid rock, and halted. Slipping from the saddle of the heaving sorrel, he dropped back a dozen yards to a huge boulder that stood out away from the edge of the trees. He climbed to the top and there, after his own rapid breathing had calmed, listened in the darkness.

Somewhere, far to the south, a pair of coyotes were setting up a wild chorus. An owl hooted into the blackness and a rain frog chirped his warning of more storms to come. There was nothing else.

If Crawford and the others had swung off the trail as he had done, it seemed logical to expect some sign, some noise that would indicate their approach. He could hear nothing. He remained perched on the rock for another quarter hour while the light of a pale moon rising above the low hills to the east grew stronger, and then gave up. He dropped to the ground and made his way back to the sorrel.

He mounted at once. He would take no chances, not with his life and Walt Woodward's twenty thousand dollars, although all indications were that he had thrown the outlaws off his trail. He would continue on for another hour at least, and make camp. Thus he would put a safe distance between himself and Crawford.

He found a good camping place a few miles, and a long hour, farther along. It was a shallow cave hollowed by wind and rain, from the face of a high butte.

A cautious man, even when he felt reasonably certain he was in the clear, he built no fire and left the sorrel saddled and ready to ride. He gave his precautions no thought, simply doing these things from instinct, and perhaps from a smattering of habit, for in the *Barranca Negra* a man learned to hold himself in readiness for an emergency at all times, or else he was not destined for a long life.

And that Ben Jordan hoped to enjoy in this new land across which he was riding. He intended to live, to take on this fine job his father's old friend, Tom Ashburn, had offered him, and no outside influence in the guise of four hard case outlaws, was going to prevent him doing so. He had been sucked into something he would have gladly avoided, if there had been a choice, but since there was not he would now see it through to the finish. And he would stay alive.

Using Woodward's blanket roll he made himself as comfortable as possible in the cave. The night was cold, the ground hard and his hunger was still far from satisfied, but he took it in stride. All things came to an end, eventually, he had learned, and tomorrow he would likely reach a settlement where he could stuff himself with a good meal, rest on a soft bed, and perhaps—

Ben Jordan came awake suddenly. An unusual noise had prodded his senses to wakefulness, setting small flags of danger waving in his mind.

He lay still for a long minute, his ears tuned to the darkness, hand gripping the butt of his revolver. It could have been a prowling animal, possibly the sorrel. He heard it again—the sharp, metallic click of iron against rock. It was the sound of an approaching horse.

Crawford!

Jordan sat up instantly. It was black as jet inside the cave, only a little better beyond in the feeble moonlight. Clouds had begun to pile up and were scudding swiftly across the sky, gathering for more rain.

Picking up the saddlebags and blanket, Ben moved into the open. He took each step with extreme care as he worked his way toward the sorrel picketed fifty feet or so to the left. Almost there, he raised himself to full height and glanced toward the stand of oak brush, seeking to pinpoint the horse's exact position. He saw the silhouette of the gelding, and at the same instant heard a man's hushed voice speak.

'There's his horse. It's him, sure enough. I'd know that sorrel anywhere.'

There was a brief silence and a second voice said: 'Where you reckon he is?'

'Hunkered up against that cliff, I expect. Bart and Cleve are movin' in from that side. Smart thing for us to do is set tight. He'll make a run for the horse.'

'Just what I was figurin'.'

Ben remained crouched behind a clump of brush, listening, waiting, trying to think of a plan, a means for escape. Crawford and the one called Cleve Aaron were sneaking up to the cave, according to what he had just heard. That placed them behind him now. Gates and Arlie Davis would be the two hiding in the darkness ahead, blocking his course to the gelding. He could not drop back—and he could not go on...

'Gates?'

'Yeh?'

'Just can't figure it out. Know damn well I plugged that jasper. Hit him square—but here he is, ridin' just like nothin' had happened.'

'Maybe you just thought you got him.'

'You seen the blood, same as me.'

'Sure, but it could have been a flesh wound, somethin' that didn't do much damage.'

'Don't make sense. I seen him grab at his chest, dang near fall off'n his horse—'

'Then who the hell we been follerin', his ghost?' Gates demanded impatiently. 'We seen him ridin', and we know he's around here somewhere. Ain't that proof enough you didn't wing him?'

'But I know I—'

'Forget it, and keep your trap shut for a bit. We don't want him findin' out we're hidin' here.'

The fact that he was riding Woodward's sorrel was not the only reason they were mistaking him for the man, Ben thought with a tight smile. He was wearing the sheepskin jacket that had been Woodward's, also. Recognizing it wiped all doubts from their minds.

His thoughts came to an abrupt halt. A sound back in the direction of the cave brought him sharply to the moment. Crawford and Aaron would break out into the open soon. They would discover the cave was empty, and press on toward the sorrel. He must move, and move fast or else become trapped in a deadly game of hide and seek.

He raised himself again, swept the surrounding brush with a probing glance. Gates and Arlie Davis were somewhere to his left, on a direct line between him and the gelding, judging from their voices. If he could circle wide, come in to the sorrel from the far side...

It was worth a try. He moved off at once, keeping low and taking time to create no sound. Every few yards he paused, listened, and now and then he would search out the silhouette of the big horse to be certain he was not going too far.

Inch by inch, it seemed to Ben Jordan, he made the circle. He had heard no more sounds back at the cave and Gates and Davis were remaining stone silent. He crept on, always fearful the saddlebags would scrape against the brush and betray him, or that he would put his weight upon a dry branch, and create a loud popping noise that would be heard by all four of the outlaws.

But finally he completed the arc. He was in front of the sorrel now, and could approach the horse head on. He hunched forward, and rested himself on his elbows, breathing hard. It had been a tiring effort, but he had been lucky. He had not aroused Gates and Arlie Davis. He turned his head toward the cave, disturbed because there had been no sounds from Crawford and Aaron. Were they still there, or had they closed in? Were they also standing watch over the sorrel?

He resumed the tedious crawl, reaching a point where he dared advance no further. His sudden appearance was certain to startle the horse, and cause him to shy and draw the attention of the outlaws. He considered that, but could find no answer to it. He had to gain the gelding's side, and jerk the short tether rope free and get on the saddle.

His hand touched a rock, one the size of his fist. He picked it up, a thought racing into his mind. If he could turn the outlaw's attention to another direction for only a few moments... He drew himself to a crouch, made ready to race to the sorrel. He cocked his arm, threw the rock toward the cave.

The instant it struck, setting up a loud, dry clatter, Jordan surged toward the gelding.

The horse saw him and jerked back. Ben seized the tail of the tie rope with his left hand and pulled, gathering the reins with his right, all in one motion. He vaulted onto the shying sorrel's back, and fought to bring the frightened animal under control.

'Hey—here! He's over here!'

It was Gates' surprised voice. Jordan ignored the nearness of it, and sawed at the bit to bring the gelding about to head him off and away from the outlaws.

'Over here! Over here!' Gates yelled again.

Jordan got the sorrel pointed right, sent him plunging recklessly down the slope, praying he would not stumble and fall, would not run straight into a canyon or a dead end.

A gun blasted through the darkness. Another. Someone was yelling—Crawford probably—shouting for the others to keep shooting, for someone to bring the horses, to watch the sorrel, not lose him.

A fresh volley of gunshots smashed through the night, and set up a chain of rolling echoes. Jordan bent low over the saddle, urged the gelding on. The big horse responded with a burst of speed, then suddenly began to slow. The dark formation of a bluff loomed directly ahead, blocking his path.

Desperately, Jordan cut to his right. A stand of scrub oak barred the sorrel's path;

he cleared it in a long jump. Guns blazed through the darkness immediately. Jordan realized the outlaws had spotted him, and were now rushing down slope, trying to head him off. He hammered at the sorrel's flanks for more speed. The big gelding seemed to sink lower as he lengthened his stride.

And then Ben Jordan felt the sudden, solid jolt of a bullet driving into his left arm, just below the shoulder. He sagged forward in the saddle, shocked by the impact. He grabbed for the horn and hung on.

CHAPTER FIVE

The sorrel plunged heedlessly through the rock and brush for a good half mile, finally broke out onto wide, grass covered flats. By some miracle he had not fallen although there had been three or four times when the big red horse had stumbled, but always he had recovered and raced on.

Near the center point of the plain they intersected a road. It was little more than paralleling trails in the pale moonlight, but Jordan swung the gelding onto it, and they rushed on through the night, the horse running free and easy over the smooth, spongy ground. Ben threw a glance over his shoulder.

The outlaws were in pursuit. Two followed the route he had taken, the other pair were higher on the slope, keeping pace with him. But he had a good quarter mile lead and the sorrel showed no indication of slowing.

Jordan settled down to a race. His arm was beginning to pain him now that the anesthesia of shock was wearing off. He examined the wound as best he could. The bullet had struck just below the bone, had passed entirely through the fleshy part of his arm. It had bled considerably and Jordan further stanched the steady oozing by cramming his handkerchief inside his sleeve and forcing it about the openings in a makeshift pressure bandage. It would serve until he could get the outlaws off his heels, but he knew he must have proper medical attention soon.

He looked ahead. The road appeared to run on indefinitely, faint, twin lines of gray in the deep color of the grass that stretched northward through the half light. But the valley through which he fled seemed to be narrowing, crowding in closer to create a sort of pass. There was no possibility of Crawford and his men overtaking and blocking his flight—thanks to the sorrel—but the darkly-clothed hillsides did offer a solution to a problem that would eventually present itself.

He must rid himself of the outlaws soon, for with daylight, the men would bring their rifles into use and his lead was not sufficient to put him beyond a long gun's reach. If they failed to hit him, they would get the gelding.

He began to drift the sorrel off the road gradually angling toward the darker shadows to the right. It would be slower going over the rougher ground but the sacrifice of speed would be well worth while, if his plan worked. The break in the horse's stride immediately sent shooting pains stabbing through Jordan's injured arm, but he clenched his teeth and rode on; if luck were still with him it would soon be over.

When he was well off the road, he pressed the sorrel to a faster pace, hoping his disappearance from the open had worked its desired effect. He looked back. He could not see the two men who had been behind him on the flats because of the long shadows, but the pair high up on the slope were now swinging down, hurrying to rejoin their companions.

Jordan grinned tightly. So far it was going as he had expected. He wanted Crawford and the others to believe he had cut off and was seeking a hiding place somewhere on the hillside. While they were thus diverted, searching about for him, unsure whether he had actually turned off or not, he would continue on through the pass. If he could make his way through, relying on darkness to cover his movements, he would gain precious time.

He reached the foot of the slope that led upward to the narrow gash between the two hills. Here the good fortune he had hoped for was evident; the shoulders of the road were brushy, shot with deep shadows. Keeping within the wild growth, he gained the crest and halted.

He looked back. There was no sign of the outlaws. They had taken the bait, and were now somewhere in the trees on the rock-strewn hillside miles below hunting for him.

Jordan sighed in weary relief and walked the tired sorrel through the opening, thankful he had not actually sought to escape back in the valley for one man, posted in the pass, could have effectively blocked his way with no difficulty when he did attempt to ride through.

The gelding fell into an easy lope down the grade, again staying to the smooth surface of the road. Now and then Jordan twisted about on his saddle for a look at the slice in the summit of the ridge but when, an hour later, he saw no indication of Crawford and his men, he concluded that he had finally shaken them, and he worried no more about the matter.

Near dawn he broke out of the rolling

foothills onto another wide flat. On the far side he saw smoke trails winding into the morning sky and recognized the low, blurred outlines of a settlement. Somewhat faint from the loss of blood and lack of food, and groggy for sleep, he struck out across the alkali-streaked plain.

When he reached the outskirts of the town, a cluster of two dozen or so buildings strung out on either side of a single street, he halted and glanced over his shoulder, the old inborn caution still very much alert with him. No riders were in sight. Crawford and his friends were yet beyond the pass, he guessed.

But eventually they would realize he had tricked them, and would resume the chase. They would reach the town, make their inquiries and likely make a house to house search. Accordingly, he must move with care. It would be smart to by-pass the settlement entirely, but this he could not do; his arm needed attending to, and he must have food.

Jordan circled to the rear of the first structure. A man, chopping wood, glanced up at his approach, eying him with frank curiosity.

Ben halted the sorrel. 'There a doctor around here?'

The man studied him. 'You hurt?'

Jordan, keeping his blood stained shoulder

turned from the man, said, 'Friend of mine got himself shot up pretty bad. Ought to take the doc to him.'

The man nodded. 'Sure. Doc's place is right on down the street. Third house from the end, on this side.'

'Obliged,' Jordan murmured, and moved on.

He located the physician's residence, still keeping to the rear of the buildings, and rode into the yard. A small barn stood at the back of the lot and, not hesitating, he guided the sorrel into it, halted him in one of the empty stalls. Two other horses were under the roof and a buggy was parked near the doorway.

He threw an armload of hay into the manger, and bucketed out a quantity of grain for the gelding, and then headed for the house with Woodward's saddlebags slung across his good shoulder. He felt oddly light-headed and he was unsteady on his feet, but he managed to reach the door.

At his knock a thin, elderly man wearing dark trousers, vest, a striped shirt with no collar attached, peered at him through steel-rimmed spectacles.

'Yes? I'm Doctor Hensley. What's the trouble?'

'My arm,' Jordan replied. 'Needs some fixing up.'

Hensley continued to stare. 'I'd guess you could stand something to eat, too. And a little sleep.' He stepped back, holding the door open. 'Come on in.'

Jordan followed the physician through the quiet house to his office quarters fronting the street. Hensley pointed to an iron and worn leather examining table.

'Sit there. And peel off that jacket and shirt,' he said, and left the room.

Ben stripped to the waist, doing it slowly, painfully. By the time he was ready the doctor was back, bringing a water tumbler half filled with whiskey.

'Drink this,' he ordered, handing the glass to Ben, and began to examine the wound. 'Nice. Clean. You're lucky, mister. Didn't even nick the bone.'

Jordan nodded, downed the liquor. It struck him like a small thunderbolt, but he began to feel better almost at once as tension faded from his long body and relaxation set in.

'Lay back,' Hensley said, taking the empty glass. 'Take me a few minutes to dress this, then I'll stir you up a cup of coffee.' He paused, smiled down at Ben. 'When did you say you'd eaten last?'

'Didn't mention it,' Jordan answered, 'but it's been a couple of days since I had a full meal.'

'See what I can do about that, too,' the doctor said, turning to a cabinet filled with bottles of medicine.

37

Stretched out on the table and lulled by the whiskey, Jordan felt drowsiness creeping over him. He struggled against it for a few minutes, and finally gave in.

Ben awoke with Hensley shaking him insistently. He was still on the table but the medicine man was finished with his arm. He moved it experimentally. There was only slight pain and a bit of stiffness.

Hensley said, 'How does it feel?'

'Fine,' Jordan replied. He turned his head toward the chair where his shirt and jacket had been hung. Woodward's saddlebags were there. He shifted his eyes then to the window. The sun was still bright and a pall of dust hung in the street. 'How long have I been asleep?'

'Couple of hours. Dead to the world. How about some coffee?'

'Could sure use it,' Ben said, sitting up. The abrupt motion set his senses to spinning. He hung there, face tipped down, the strong, pungent smell of medicine in his nostrils, allowed the giddiness to pass. When it was gone he grinned wryly at the doctor.

'Guess I moved a little too quick.'

'You'll be all right in a few minutes. You need something in your belly, more than anything. There's a restaurant down the street.' The physician paused, studied Ben thoughtfully. 'Any reason why you can't use it?'

Jordan said, 'No, reckon not. But until then I'll sure appreciate some coffee.'

Hensley wheeled, disappeared into the interior of the house. He returned in a few moments carrying a thick mug of black coffee and a plate of sweet rolls.

'This ought to hold you until you can get to that restaurant,' he said.

He placed the food on a table near the window and stood back as Jordan settled on a chair and began to eat. The whiskey was still having its way with him, but the steaming coffee and rolls would quickly dull its effects.

When he had finished the first cup and was sipping at the second, Hensley said, 'Would have let you sleep longer but saw some men ride into town. They've been parading around like they were looking for somebody. They friends of yours?'

Jordan sat his cup on the table quietly, felt the tautness begin to build within him once again. It could be Crawford and his men. If they had not spent too much time searching for him before they realized they had been tricked, they could have arrived. Or it could be someone else—riders who happened to be strangers to the doctor.

After a moment Ben said, 'Doubt it. How many in the party?'

Hensley said, 'Four.'

Ben stiffened as granite-hard tension

closed in about him completely. Four men, that tallied. Still it could be coincidence...

'They stop here?'

Hensley turned, replaced two or three bottles in the cabinet. He shook his head. 'No. Like I said, they've just been riding up and down the street. Appear to be hunting for somebody.' He glanced out the window. 'Fact is, here they come again.'

Jordan swung about, threw his gaze into the dusty pall suspended between the buildings. It was Bart Crawford and his three hard-faced companions.

CHAPTER SIX

Crawford, a dark, grim man with a square-cornered jaw, rode center and slightly in front of the others. To his left was Aaron, hat pushed to the back of his head revealing a shock of brick red hair. The one on the gray horse was Gates, a sallow faced man who looked as though he would be more at home at a faro table than on a saddle. At the near end of the line, and apparently the youngest of the crowd, was Arlie Davis. He was easing himself by leaning forward in the stirrups while his eyes, like the rest, probed along the street in a ceaseless quest.

'They looking for you?' Hensley asked

quietly.

Jordan waited, watched until the outlaws had passed the house and were moving slowly on toward the end of the street. He said then, 'Reckon so but they're not friends.'

'They the reason for that bullet hole in your arm?'

Ben nodded. He was considering the advisability of taking the physician into his confidence, of perhaps going to the town marshal and asking his protection. Immediately he knew it would be a bad move, and far too risky. The local lawman could prove to be of little help, unable to stand up against such men as Bart Crawford and the others. And he was reluctant to involve the physician or anyone else in his trouble.

Besides, he had made his promise to Walt Woodward that he would personally see to the delivery of the money. To bring in others would only serve to complicate the problem.

Jordan rose, pulled on his shirt and brush jacket. He looped the saddlebags over his shoulder. There was the faint clink of coins as the pouches slapped against his body. Hensley's expression did not alter.

'How much do I owe you, doc?'

The physician shrugged. 'Couple of dollars will do it. Sure you can ride?'

Jordan said, 'I'm sure,' and handed over

the specified amount. 'Put my horse in your barn and fed him when I first rode in. Owe you for that, too.'

'Forget it,' Hensley said. 'Lot of people around here pay me off with hay and grain. Always got plenty.' He glanced toward the street. 'Here they come again. Which way you headed?'

Jordan studied the medical man thoughtfully as if considering the wisdom of a reply. Finally he said, 'North, or I guess you'd say north-east.'

Hensley said, 'Give them five minutes and they'll be at the other end of town. Then pull out and they won't spot you.'

'Obliged to you,' Ben said, and started for the door. He paused. 'Anybody asks, I'll appreciate your saying you haven't seen me.'

The medical man shook his head. 'If it's the marshal I'll have to tell him the truth. Matter of principle. Anybody else wants to know it's none of their damn business.'

'Good enough,' Jordan said and moved on.

He crossed to the barn, backed the gelding out of his stall and mounted. Pulling up to the door he halted. After several moments he rode from the yard, again keeping close to the buildings until he reached the end of the line, and there angled off toward the north.

He veered to the right, putting himself from view of anyone on the street. If

Crawford and his men made another return sweep and glanced on ahead, they would undoubtedly see him, at least they would see a horseman riding toward the north. If he could put enough distance between himself and the settlement there would be a question in their minds as to whether he was the man they sought, or was just another rider crossing the flats. He could only hope that he would be far enough away to create that question when the moment came.

But luck was not with him this time. Shortly after noon, as he was nearing the far side of the flats, he saw the outlaws on the road behind him. They had just emerged from the settlement, appearing only as small, dark shapes in the distance. Yet there was no doubt as to their identity.

Either they had discovered he had been in the town and ridden on, or else they were simply assuming such would be the fact since it was the only course left open to him. Most likely, however, some citizen had noted his passage and, when asked, volunteered the information. That they would have learned nothing from Doc Hensley Ben was dead certain.

He began to look ahead, hoping for some means once more to throw them off his trail. It was yet hours until darkness, and night promised little salvation anyway. It had not turned the outlaws aside before. There was little reason to expect it would now.

At the end of the plain a finger of trees extending down from the hills formed a dark, green barrier and Ben hurried the sorrel to gain that shelter as quickly as possible. Once inside he would be lost to view insofar as Crawford was concerned, and if he so desired he could then alter his directions and thereby confuse the outlaws.

A vast cloud of dust rising above the hills to his left drew Jordan's attention a quarter hour later and set him to thinking. From all indications it was a cattle drive. It was late in the summer for such, but a man didn't always follow the pattern, and likely there was some particular reason for it. Regardless, it presented a possibility; why not join the herd, perhaps take on a job of riding—long enough to sidetrack Crawford and his men?

He swung off the road at once, slanted toward the yellowish pall. Two hours later he caught up with the drive, one of fair size moving slowly toward the east. He sought out the trail boss, a man named Slaughter, he was told by a dust plastered cowhand.

Slaughter was a huge man. He rode heavily in the saddle. His face was sweaty and also well caked with dust although he was in front of the cattle when Jordan finally found him. He favored Ben with a hard, irritable glance.

'Now, what in the hell's on your mind?' he

demanded.

Jordan grinned. A contrary herd had a way of getting under a man's hide. 'Looking for a job. How you fixed for trail hands?'

Slaughter swore. 'What I got ain't worth the powder it'd take to blow them off a bunk! Lump the whole bunch together and a man wouldn't have one good cowpuncher. That's how I'm fixed! You handle cows before?'

'Longhorns. Since I was big enough to climb onto a saddle.'

'You're hired,' Slaughter said bluntly. 'Fall back to swing, on the north side. Tuck's havin' trouble. Can't seem to keep the critters caught up with the rest. See if you can straighten it out.'

Jordan nodded and wheeled away, inwardly satisfied. This should throw Crawford off his heels. The outlaws would never think to swing wide of the road and check a trail herd; they would believe him still ahead of them somewhere in the darkness. He would help Slaughter for a day and then ride on. He should have no more trouble now.

He found Tuck, a squat, moon-faced young rider at the edge of the herd. Two more cowhands were moving about and all were having their problems with the steers which were continually bolting from the sea of heaving bodies and making a run for the brushy slopes of the hills a short distance away.

'You a new hand?' Tuck asked, mopping at his ruddy features.

Jordan said, 'Yeh. Slaughter sent me over to give you some help.'

'Need it,' the puncher said. 'Orneriest bunch of bones and hide I ever seen!'

'Think I see what's causing it,' Ben said, his eyes on an old blue-nosed gray longhorn that seemed bent on shaping up a herd all his own. 'Bear down on 'em, push 'em hard,' he said, and spurred the gelding toward the old mossy-horn.

He wheeled in close to the gray, and began to haze him from the herd. The activity aroused the pain in his injured arm but he gave it no attention, concentrating on driving the big steer away from the herd and off toward the hills. The remainder of the cattle swept on. Tuck wheeled back to Jordan's side.

'What's the deal?' he asked, watching the gray amble off into the brush.

'He's the one holding you back,' Ben said. 'We get rid of him, we'll have no more trouble.'

Tuck frowned, scratched at his neck. 'Slaughter ain't goin' to like losin' even one lousy steer.'

'Won't lose him,' Jordan said. 'Watch.'

Just within the fringe of brush the longhorn halted, wheeled about. Head swung low, he stared at the passing herd, unhindered now by his presence. He shook himself, bellowed his summons, but the cattle moved on unheeding. The old gray watched for several minutes, occasionally bawling his displeasure, and then finally he gave it up and began to follow.

Tuck grinned at Jordan. 'You some kin to these danged tick farms?'

'About as close as I can be without being one of them,' Ben replied. 'He'll catch up when we haul in for the night. If he tries the same stunt tomorrow, we'll run him off again.'

The puncher spat dust. 'Might be better to put a bullet in his head and tell Slaughter the coyotes got him.' He reached for his canteen, unscrewed the cap and offered it to Jordan. 'You signin' on for the whole drive?'

Ben took a swallow of water. 'No, heading on north. Going to work for Ashburn on the Lazy A.'

'Too bad,' Tuck said. 'We can use a man with your kind of savvy.'

It was full dark when they bedded the herd for the night. They were still west of the road Jordan had been following and his guess was that the outlaws had long since passed that point and were miles beyond. It would be smart to stick with Slaughter and his trail herd for another full day, Ben decided. By then Crawford and his bunch would be well out of the way.

Slaughter rode by, passing the word that half the crew was to stay on watch while the remainder went in for the evening meal at the camp. Jordan waved Tuck toward the chuck wagon, electing to be one of those who waited, and it was near nine o'clock when the round-faced rider returned to relieve him.

He swung off through the night toward the blazing campfire where the cook had set up his kitchen. He hoped he would be one of those chosen to take the late turn at night-hawking as he was beginning to feel the need of rest and sleep. If he could have only four or five hours on a bedroll he would be good as new again.

He had made up his mind to ask Slaughter for just such an arrangement but as he drew near the camp his eyes caught sight of riders halted at the edge of the broad circle of light thrown by the leaping flames.

He swung in behind the chuck wagon quickly, his face going taut, his muscles beginning to tighten as a wild suspicion ripped through him. When he was a few yards from the canvas-topped vehicle, he stopped the sorrel and dismounted. At a crouch, he eased in silently, careful not to stumble and not to draw the attention of any of the men in the camp. He reached the wagon, knelt down and glanced through the spokes of a wheel.

A wave of exasperation, almost desperation, moved through him. The riders, still on their horses, were only too familiar; Crawford and his three followers.

CHAPTER SEVEN

The outlaws faced Slaughter. The big trail boss stood with his legs spread, his back to Jordan. Several of his riders had gathered about him in careless but watchful silence.

'What's got you thinkin' he came here?' Slaughter demanded, blunt and impatient.

'Not sure he did,' Crawford replied. 'Just had a hunch he might. Man on the run trys all kinds of fancy tricks.'

He had not fooled the outlaws for a solitary moment, Ben realized. Crawford, personally acquainted with the problems of a man on the dodge, had recognized the possibilities a trail herd presented and deemed it wise not to ignore but to investigate.

'A tall man, wearin' a sheepskin jacket. Rides a sorrel with white forelegs.'

Slaughter was still for several moments. 'What do you want him for?'

'Bank robbery,' Crawford said. 'Been chasin' him clear across Arizona and half of

New Mexico. About had him two or three times, but he's mighty slippery. Got away from us.'

Jordan listened in amazement to the bald effrontery of Bart Crawford. The outlaws were passing themselves off as lawmen! They were making it appear that he—or, in reality, Walt Woodward—was the criminal! A surge of anger rocked Ben Jordan. He started to rise, to rush out into the open and confront Crawford and his gang, denounce them as liars before Slaughter and the others.

And then he realized it would be a foolish gesture. He could prove nothing. He was a stranger to the trail boss and his riders, and it would be his word against that of Bart Crawford, backed by Aaron, Davis and the narrow-faced Gates. Slaughter would have little choice but to believe Crawford. And he did have twenty thousand dollars in his saddlebags, something that would bolster Crawford's accusations despite any explanation he would make. Fuming, feeling utterly helpless to protect himself, Ben Jordan listened to the conversation between the two men.

'Figure he's shot up some,' Crawford said, 'One of my boys here thinks he winged him a couple of days ago.'

'Man I hired didn't look like anything was botherin' him,' Slaughter stated flatly. 'Fact is, he—'

'Was a place on his sleeve,' a puncher sprawled out on his bedroll, propped on one elbow, volunteered. Ben recognized him as the first man he had encountered when he reached the herd.

'What kind of a place?'

'Sort of ragged like. Maybe a bullet hole. And somebody's washed it up, like they'd cleaned off blood.'

Crawford glanced at Cleve Aaron, then at Gates and Davis. 'Could've been him,' he drawled. 'What kind of a horse was he ridin'?'

There was no immediate answer. The puncher sank back onto his blankets. Slaughter drew a sack of tobacco and a folder of papers from a pocket, and began to roll himself a smoke.

'I'm askin' what kind of a horse?' Crawford snarled. 'Speak up! You want me to charge the whole bunch of you with interferin' with the law?'

The trail boss shrugged. 'Do what you damn well please, friend. Threatenin' won't get you nowheres. I don't figure the man I hired is the one you're lookin' for.'

'What kind of a horse?' Crawford pressed in a cold voice.

'He was ridin' a sorrel,' the man on the blanket said. 'Had white stockin's.'

Gates and the other two outlaws drew themselves upright in their saddles, looking expectantly at Crawford.

'Where is he?' the renegade leader asked.

Slaughter waved his hand toward the swale where the herd was bedded. 'Out doin' his trick at nighthawkin'. He'll be comin' in for supper pretty quick.'

Arlie Davis, breaking the silence he and the others had maintained throughout the conversation, said, 'Reckon, we'd better get over there. Could be he'll pull out again.'

Crawford thought for a moment, shook his head. 'Nope, don't figure he'll do that. He thinks he's safe here. And tryin' to find him in the dark could tip him off. Best we wait.' He brought his attention back to the men around the fire, touched each with his hard glance. 'Nobody leaves understand? Anybody tries to warn him—'

'Won't be anybody doin' that,' Slaughter said, 'because we don't figure he's your man. Jacobs there's got his ropes all crossed up about the puncher he saw.' The trail boss paused, confronted with extending a standard courtesy he cared little to observe in this instance. 'Reckon you might as well step down. Coffee and grub over there at the chuck wagon.'

Slaughter turned away. Crawford's voice, sharp and suspicious, split the hush. 'Where you think you're goin'?'

The cattleman did not halt, simply glanced over his shoulder. 'I'm takin' a turn around the herd, then I'm crawlin' into my blankets.'

Crawford spurred his black across the camp and pulled up short in front of the trail boss. 'What I said goes for you, too, mister!'

Slaughter, a man with temper always lying close to the surface, reached up impulsively. He grasped the front of Crawford's coat, dragged him from the saddle. He swung the outlaw half around, shoved him, and sent him sprawling into the dust.

'Don't be tellin' me what I can't do!' Slaughter raged. 'Happens to be my camp, and you, lawman or not, sure ain't runnin' things here!'

Davis and Cleve Aaron had moved quickly, and were now at opposite ends of the circle thrown by the firelight. Gates was motionless. Each now held a cocked pistol. In the tight silence Bart Crawford pulled himself to his feet, his eyes on Slaughter's huge shape. He hung there, half crouched, poised as though ready to spring. And then he relaxed suddenly. He picked up his hat, dusted himself.

'I'll overlook that, mister,' he said in a low voice. 'This time, anyway. But you're not ridin' out. You or nobody else—not until Woodward shows up. After that you can do as you damn please.'

A man on the opposite side of the fire cleared his throat nervously. 'Cattle's a mite jumpy, Mr Slaughter,' he said. 'Some sort of a ruckus would sure start them a runnin'.'

The big trail boss glanced at the threatening figures of Gates, Arlie Davis and Aaron. He shrugged angrily. 'All right, all right. Have it your way.'

Jordan watched Slaughter wheel and cross the camp to where a lantern hung from a mesquite bush. There the trail boss squatted down, drew a tally book from his pocket and began to flip through the pages.

Crawford studied the man in glowering silence for several moments, and then turned to the rest of his party. He motioned and they drew together again and dismounted.

Ben Jordan withdrew into the shadows as the four outlaws started across the camp for the chuck wagon behind which he was crouching. The cook, hunched by the fire, sucked at his blackened pipe, and made no effort to rise and accommodate the guests; common courtesy required Slaughter to invite the strangers to climb down and eat, but it did not necessarily include being waited on.

Jordan reached the sorrel, and stood for a time with his eyes on the camp. The tough, brassy ways of Bart Crawford had infuriated him. He would like nothing better than to call the outlaw's bluff, and expose him and his three men for what they were. He could imagine Slaughter's irate reaction.

But it wasn't practical, or even possible. He had nothing with which to back his contention. He could do nothing but let the matter drop—and move on.

He took up the gelding's reins and led the horse away from the camp a good distance before he swung to the saddle. He could take no chances on Crawford, or anyone else, hearing the sound of the sorrel's hoofbeats. He glanced to the stars in the black canopy of sky overhead, squared his directions, and struck off once again into the north-east. Tom Ashburn's Lazy A spread could not be far now.

CHAPTER EIGHT

Two days later Ben Jordan found himself near his destination.

He had seen the landscape change gradually from high, rugged mountains with towering peaks and deep canyons, to endless, rolling plateaus, rich with grass and gentle to look upon. Far to the east a new range of hills had appeared, seemingly more massive than those through which he had traveled, and so distant they were only a bluish smudge on the horizon.

But the Lazy A would be found in a wide valley, he had been told when he chanced upon an itinerant peddler of housewares, and the mountains to the east were another world. Tom Ashburn's ranch was a fine place, with good buildings, plenty of shade provided by giant cottonwoods, and all the clear, cold water it could ever use. In fact, the Lazy A was the finest spread in the territory, as was also Tom Ashburn the finest of men!

The peddler had been right, at least so far, Ben thought as he topped out a low rise near the middle of the afternoon and started down a slope that led to the ranch. The house was a long, well kept structure, neatly painted and trimmed and further beautified by a wealth of vines and flowers. Huge, spreading trees, vivid gold now in the crisp fall air, overshadowed it all.

Several corrals and a small garden plot lay to the rear of the main building, while other structures, the bunkhouse, wagonshed, barns and the like stood off to one side. A small pond a short distance beyond those mirrored the sun and, looking more closely, Jordan could see several canals cutting away from its circular shape to form other convenient water holes.

Water, that was the answer, Ben thought, remembering the scarcity of such in the *Barranca Negra*. If a man had plenty of water, he could grow anything. How many times had he heard his father make that statement? And how many times had he, personally, realized its truth? It was the key to success, to life itself in the vast, frontier west and a man rose or fell according to the supply available to him. But it was a problem that would never plague Tom Ashburn. In one glance Ben saw the glitter of a half a dozen springs surging up among the cottonwoods, all independent of the distant pond.

As he rode below the rim, Jordan cast a final look over his shoulder at his back trail, a gesture that had become habit with him since his first encounter with Bart Crawford and his men. The endless flats were empty and the comforting thought settled in his mind that at last he had shaken the outlaws, that, with a modicum of luck, he never again would see them.

And the time was near when he could deliver Walt Woodward's money to his widow and discharge that obligation. The saddlebags with their store of currency and gold coins had become a wearisome burden since he had accepted them and he would be thankful to rid himself of the responsibility.

He circled Ashburn's house, came into it from the front. Two men and two women stood on the gallery that crossed its width. They glanced up as he swung in and slanted toward the hitchrack. The older of the men stepped off the porch immediately, a quick smile cracking his weathered face. He extended a heavily veined hand.

'Ben Jordan, sure as a mule's got long ears!' he shouted. 'Ain't seen you in ten, twelve year, but I'd know you anywhere. You're the spittin' image of your pa!'

Ben dropped from the sorrel and enclosed the old rancher's fingers in his own. He did not remember Ashburn too well, for he only faintly recalled the man's long ago visit to the *Barranca Negra*. But he said, 'Good to see you again, Mr Ashburn.'

'Mister Ashburn!' the rancher echoed. 'I'm Tom to you, boy!' He stepped back, a lean, bent man with faded eyes and seamy face. His hair and drooping mustache were snow white. 'Come on and meet the rest of the family.'

Ben hung Woodward's saddlebags across his shoulder and followed the rancher to the porch. Ashburn seized him by the arm.

'Folks, this here's Dave Jordan's boy, Ben. He's who I've been waitin' for. My wife, Ellie,' he added, nodding to the older woman who smiled gravely and shook Jordan's hand. 'My daughter, Sally.'

Ben's glance had been drawn to the girl from the start. She was young, well built and had light brown hair and blue eyes that had a bright, dancing quality to them. She took his hand in a firm grasp.

'I'm pleased to know you, Ben Jordan.'

Ben swallowed, bobbed his head, suddenly conscious of his appearance, of his awkwardness in her presence. But he managed a grin, said, 'My pleasure...'

'Feller there is Oran Bishop,' Ashburn went on, turning to the young puncher waiting quietly off to one side. 'He's been sort of fillin' in for you, until you got here.'

Bishop was a man with about the same number of years behind him as Ben, twenty-four. He was a husky, six foot blond, handsome in a rugged sort of way. He was fairly well dressed. He took Jordan's hand and said, 'Howdy,' in a cool voice that carried no promise of friendship.

'Reckon you've been quite a spell in the saddle,' Ashburn said when the introductions were over. 'Long ride up from Mexico. Have any trouble findin' the place?'

Ben said, 'None. Met a wagon peddler. Put me on the right road.'

'Good. Didn't figure you'd have any problems. I been around here so long now most everybody knows where the Lazy A is.' He wheeled to Bishop. 'Oran, expect you'd better go move your duds and gear out of the foreman's cabin. Ben'll be wantin' to settle in.' He came back to Jordan. 'You got a wife, maybe some family that'll be comin' along later?'

Ben shook his head. 'No, I'm all there is to it.' He glanced at Bishop. 'No need for you to move out. We can share the quarters.'

Bishop said, 'No thanks, I'll get back in the bunkhouse with the rest of the hands.'

There was a trace of bitterness in the man's voice and Ben realized resentment lay strong in his mind. Likely he had expected to step in and fill the job of ramrod for the Lazy A when the opportunity arose. That he would exhibit little cordiality to an outsider was to be expected.

Jordan gave that a moment's consideration and shrugged it off. He regretted Bishop's attitude but he could not allow it to matter. Had Tom Ashburn felt the man capable he would have selected him for the foreman's job and not sent all the way to the *Barranca Negra* for a stranger.

Ashburn said, 'I'll show you around the place. You can meet the rest of the crew tonight.' In his quick way, he wheeled to Bishop. 'Oran, you take Ben's horse and turn him over to the wrangler. Put his stuff in the cabin. Forgot to ask,' he added, turning back to Ben. 'You eat yet, boy?'

Jordan said, 'I'll do until supper.'

'Good. Now, figure to eat your meals with us here in the main house. Like to have my foreman around where I can yammer at him.'

Ben slid a glance at Bishop. That such an arrangement did not set well with him was apparent. Probably he had been enjoying that privilege to the moment; now he was being relegated to the general dining quarters where he would take his meals with the remainder of the hands. Again Ben Jordan shook off the problem. It was something he could not worry about. Tom Ashburn was calling the shots.

Bishop reached forward. 'The saddlebags,' he said irritably. 'Pass them over if you want me to put them in your cabin.'

Jordan stepped away. 'Never mind. I'll just take them along.'

Bishop frowned. His eyes narrowed slightly at the rebuff. 'There something special about them?'

'Just a habit I've got,' Ben grinned, and moved off across the hard pack with Ashburn.

CHAPTER NINE

That evening when the crew had gathered for their meal, Tom Ashburn conducted Ben to the long, narrow dining hall that extended off the kitchen. All of the men would be there, except three or four staying with the herd, the rancher explained. Those he could meet later. As they walked into the room and halted at the head of the table, all conversation ceased.

'Want you to meet your new foreman,' Ashburn said. 'Name of Ben Jordan.'

The rancher made the rounds then, introducing each man individually. When he had completed the chore, he said, 'Reckon you've been wonderin' why I sent all the way to Mexico for a ramrod. One reason—I figure a man who can raise cattle, look after a farm and still keep his skin whole while doin' it in that *Barranca Negra* country, sure wouldn't have no trouble doin' a good job up here. That, and the fact that his daddy was the best damn cowman I ever knew.'

One of the crew, a slim Mexican named Cruz Rodriguez, looked up with interest. He smiled. 'The *Barranca Negra*, señor? It is a place I know well. How are the *banditos* these days?'

'They grow worse,' Jordan said with a smile. 'And there are more of them each year.'

Rodriguez shrugged. 'In Mexico if you would fill your belly regular, you must be either a *soldado* or a *bandito*. Nothing else pays well.'

Jordan laughed along with the crew. There was a great deal of truth in what the Mexican had said. 'We'll have to get together and talk about it, *amigo*,' he said. 'I grew up ducking bullets from both sides.'

He moved around the table then, shaking hands with each man, all of whom were cordial enough except Oran Bishop and another young puncher called Ross Colby who evidently was a close friend of Bishop's. Both maintained a cool, aloof attitude.

When it was finished he returned with Ashburn to the family quarters and spent another two hours listening to the rancher talk first of the old days in Missouri before Dave Jordan migrated to Mexico, and then about ranching in general. Ben had seen nothing of Sally, or Mrs Ashburn since supper, and when at last he arose, tired and in need of sleep, they still were not there. Tom Ashburn had apparently ruled them out of the evening's confab, decreeing that it was to be strictly man talk.

'We'll do some ridin' tomorrow,' the rancher said, watching Ben retrieve his saddlebags from behind a chair. 'Want you to get a good idea what the place is like. You can take over the next day.'

Ben nodded. 'Certainly the finest ranch I've ever seen.'

'Thanks,' Ashburn said, suddenly sober. 'Took a lot of blood and sweat, but it was worth it. Problem now is to keep it fine. Way it goes, it seems. Man puts in half his life buildin' somethin' good, then spends the rest tryin' to hang on to it.'

'You been having trouble?' Jordan asked, halting in the doorway.

'Not much. Little rustlin' goin' on now

and then. Got a few nesters. I figure you won't have no problem takin' care of both. Anyway, we'll jaw about it in the mornin'. Good night, son.'

'Good night,' Ben said and moved out into the cool darkness.

He made his way to the small house assigned to him, a squat, compact building that stood half way between Ashburn's main structure and the crew's bunkhouse. Apparently the previous foreman of the Lazy A had been a married man for there was kitchen equipment available as well as the usual living facilities.

After entering, Ben closed the door and dropped the latch into place. He struck a match to one of the lamps and then drew the shades. He began then to search out a suitable hiding place for Woodward's money. He could not continue to walk around with the leather pouches slung over his shoulder; already they had been cause for suspicion in Oran Bishop's mind—possibly also in that of Ashburn.

And the sooner he fulfilled his promise to Walt Woodward, the better for all concerned. Having the money was a worry and he would not rest easily until he had turned it over to Ollie Woodward. He could not afford to let it affect his position at the Lazy A. Tomorrow he would ask directions to the town of Langford, get Ashburn's permission to make the trip, and have done with it.

He prowled about the two rooms of the cabin, decided finally to place the leather pouches under a board in the floor that he managed to loosen. He completed the concealment by changing the furniture around somewhat, ending up with a small rug and a chair placed over the cache.

He had no personal belongings to place in the closet and in the drawers of the scarred dresser. What little he had owned had been lost when the buckskin had gone over the cliff high in the Mogollon Mountains. When he made his visit to Langford he would buy the items he needed—a razor, shaving and washing soap, and some extra clothing. Meanwhile he would made do as best he could.

He had just sat down on the bed and was beginning to undress for the night when he heard a knock. He arose, lifted the bar and faced Ross Colby.

'Man outside like to see you,' the young puncher said.

Jordan's first thoughts were that Bart Crawford had again caught up with him. He looked out into the dark yard. 'Only one?'

'That's right, only one.'

Ben pushed by Colby and stepped into the shadowy area that lay between his quarters and the bunkhouse. He heard the dry crunch of gravel, wheeled. He had a quick glimpse of Oran Bishop's set, angry features, and then a rock hard fist smashed into his jaw and sent him reeling to the ground.

He struck on his left shoulder, sending a wave of pain through his body as his weight crushed down upon his wounded arm. He lay quiet for several moments, aware of Bishop's taut shape standing over him. Two or three men were now coming from the bunkhouse and Ben could hear Ross Colby laughing. Anger began to build within Jordan. Ignoring the throbbing pain, he sat up.

Beyond Bishop, watching and waiting in silence, were the Mexican, Rodriguez, an old puncher, Amos Wall, and a third man he had not met. Colby still was near the doorway of the cabin from which a shaft of yellow lamplight laid an oblong onto the yard.

'Get up,' Bishop snarled. 'You're going to have to whip me, mister, to get my job!'

The blond puncher's fury was so intense his voice trembled. Ben pulled himself to his feet.

'Your job?'

'Would've been, if you hadn't come along,' Bishop said. 'I was all set—'

'That's a dang fool thing to say, Oran!' Amos Wall broke in. 'If Tom'd wanted you, he'd a picked you instead of sendin' clear to Mexico for Jordan.'

'Keep out of this, old man,' Bishop said without turning. 'We're deciding right here who'll ramrod this outfit. And when it's done with, I'm loading him on his horse and sending him back to Mexico.'

'You're a damn fool and there's no reason for this,' Jordan said then, his anger leveling off to a brittle hardness. 'So's you'll have it straight, I never asked for this job. Had no idea Ashburn even was looking for a man until I got a letter from him.'

'So you say.'

'It's the truth, but it's neither here nor there now. I like what I've seen of this place and I figure to stay. If you think you can change my mind for me, you're welcome to try.'

Bishop rushed in suddenly. He swung a quick left, missed as Jordan ducked away, tried to recover with a right. Ben blocked the blow with his left arm, gritted his teeth as fresh pain rocketed through him from his wounded shoulder, and drove his own right fist into Bishop's ear.

The puncher staggered, went to one knee, caught himself. He swore vividly, pulled himself upright.

'Another thing. Something else. You keep your eyes off Sally.'

He lunged again. Jordan, favoring his left arm, spun away, chopped a right to Oran's neck as he closed. Bishop howled and wheeled off.

From the half darkness Cruz Rodriguez' soft, accented voice said, 'I think you pick the wrong *hombre* this time, Oran.'

Ross Colby no longer laughed. He slouched against the wall of Jordan's quarters, watched with a stilled face.

'Damn you!' Bishop growled, anger now a wild surging torrent claiming him mentally and physically, 'I'm not letting you get away with this, not with anything! Don't know what it is but you're hiding something—trying to fool Tom.'

'I'm not trying to fool him, or anybody else,' Jordan said, circling warily. 'I'm here to work. Nothing else.'

'You're a liar!' Bishop shouted and once more moved in.

Ben fell back a step, was aware that his foot came up against something. He almost went down. From the tail of his eye he saw Rodriguez cross swiftly and take up a position next to Ross Colby. He realized then that Colby, endeavoring to help Bishop, had tried to trip him.

But there was no chance to do anything about that; besides, Rodriguez had apparently noticed it and was assuming the chore of keeping Colby out of the fight. He ducked beneath Bishop's swinging arms, crowded in tight and hammered a half a dozen rapid-fire blows into the blond puncher's belly.

Bishop struck out blindly, desperately. Jordan took a sharp blow to the head, another across the mouth that started a warm flow of blood from his lips. Fury broke loose within him then and, ignoring the pain in his arm, conscious of a stickiness along his side, he ripped a second flurry of fists into Bishop.

Oran began to gasp, started to fold forward. Ben straightened him up with a stinging blow to the chin. Bishop sought to turn away, his breathing coming now in loud, rasping grunts, his mouth gaped open. Jordan spun him back around with a smash to the side of his head.

Showing no mercy, paying no heed to the pain that screamed within him or the wetness that told him his wound had reopened, Ben Jordan punished Bishop without let-up. The puncher was weaving on his feet, helpless. He rocked back and forth, staggered forward, was driven back to his heels, only to be caught up again. Finally his knees began to buckle. He started to sink slowly, wilting as though his legs were made of smoke.

Ben felt hands close about his shoulders, drawing him off. Amos Wall's voice said, 'That'll do it, boy. Reckon he's had more'n enough.'

Sucking for breath, his body quivering

from the stress, Jordan allowed himself to be pulled away.

Oran Bishop lay sprawled on his back, mouth open, chest heaving. Ross Colby came forward, knelt beside him. He stared into the puncher's face. 'Get some water somebody,' he said.

One of the crew brought the bucket from the bunkhouse, dashed a quantity of its contents against Bishop's head. Oran groaned, thrashed about briefly, and opened his eyes. He lay still for several moments, and then finally struggled to a sitting position. He looked around, dazed.

'What—how—' he stammered.

'You just got hell knocked out of you,' Wall said laconically. 'And by a man with only one good arm.'

Jordan pulled away from the old puncher, dismay flooding through him. He had hoped to keep his wound a secret, thereby avoiding any speculation on the part of the crew, or by Tom Ashburn. But there was no hiding it now. The left sleeve of his shirt was soaked with blood.

Bishop got to his feet, stared. 'I told you,' he said, glancing at the small circle of men. 'He's hiding something. He's been shot.'

'Doesn't concern you, or the job,' Jordan snapped. 'It's a personal matter.'

'Personal—with the law, maybe?'

'The law had nothing to do with it.'

'Reckon it ain't none of our business, anyway,' Amos Wall broke in. 'And if you're lookin' for advice, Oran, I'd say you'd be smart to forget it.'

Bishop was silent for a few moments, then bent and picked up his hat. Pulling it on, he faced Jordan. 'Reckon this means I'm fired.'

Ben shook his head. 'You can quit if you're of the notion, but I won't fire you.'

Bishop stared, surprised and at a loss for words.

'Just one thing,' Jordan continued, 'if you stay, you do your job and keep out of my way. I'll take no more of your lip or your foolishness. Or yours,' he added swinging his glance to Ross Colby.

Colby murmured, looked down. Beside him, Ben saw Cruz Rodriguez beaming at him through the poor light, his broad teeth gleaming whitely.

'What's it to be?' he demanded, coming back to Bishop.

The blond puncher shrugged. 'I'll stay,' he said, his tone low and surly.

'Then get that chip off your shoulder and figure on doing a job, or else you are finished. You're one man I figure on watching close.'

Bishop wheeled, started for the bunkhouse. Wall stepped up to Jordan. 'Come on, boy, let's see what we can do about that arm of yours. It's bleedin' right good.'

Ben moved across the yard toward Rodriguez who stood holding open the door to his quarters. Half way he paused, turned.

'One thing more,' he said, 'there'll be nothing said about this. Not to the rest of the crew—or to Tom Ashburn... That clear?'

The men nodded. Colby said, 'It's clear,' but Oran Bishop gave no indication that he had heard, and simply walked away, morose and sullen in his defeat.

CHAPTER TEN

They prepared to ride out shortly after breakfast that next morning, Tom Ashburn, Jordan—and Sally. Ben was surprised and secretly pleased the girl was coming with them. He was finding himself more and more interested in her and had been hoping for a chance to talk to her. There had been little opportunity during the two meals they had shared.

He watched her stuff a lunch into saddlebags and swing lightly onto her pony. She rode astride, and used one of the heavy stock saddles, just as did any of the Lazy A ranch hands. She was wearing a corduroy skirt split up the center, a white shirt with a bright yellow scarf gathered about her neck.

Soft, high-heeled boots and a broad brimmed, flat crowned hat, completed her attire. As she settled herself on her pinto, Ben felt a tightness fill his throat; she made a picture he knew would never fade from his mind.

Ashburn came from the house grumbling at the stiffness of his joints, and mounted up. He cocked his head at Ben. 'Gettin' old sure as hell. Was a time when I enjoyed crawlin' out early and pilin' onto a horse. Now it's a right smart chore.'

Jordan grinned his understanding and the three of them wheeled out of the yard, the rancher and his daughter waving to Ellie Ashburn as they passed the kitchen door. They road abreast and in silence, the men flanking the girl until they were out of the hollow in which the ranch buildings lay and had gained the plateau above it.

'Told the boys to drift the lower herd on west,' Ashburn said as they broke out onto the flats. 'Lot of new grass over there. Been no grazin' on it since spring.'

'How many head you running?' Ben asked, his eyes drifting lazily over the vast expanse of gray-green. It was like a monstrous field with only a few trees scattered here and there to break the horizon.

'Pretty close to four thousand.'

Jordan whistled softly. Sally turned and

gave him her smile. Ashburn said, 'Most I've ever had. Been holdin' back on sellin'. Market's climbin'. I figure next year will be the time to turn 'em loose.'

'What's the price now?'

'Fifteen, sixteen dollars thereabouts. Ought to go to eighteen, maybe twenty by spring.'

Ben considered that for a time. On his and his father's place in the *Barranca Negra*, they had never owned as many as four hundred head of stock, much less four thousand. And the highest price he could recall having received for a steer was nine dollars.

'Big difference in ranching up here,' he said. 'How much of a herd do you figure to sell off?'

'Only the three and four year old stuff. They'll be prime, and just right for the market.'

'Wonderful country,' Ben murmured. 'Should be no problem raising cattle up here.'

'You like what you see?' Sally asked.

His eyes settled on her. 'Everything,' he said, a faint smile tugging at his lips. 'Everything.'

Sally blushed slightly and turned away.

Ashburn said, 'Swing north. Expect we ought to have a look at the line shacks up there. Recollect somebody sayin' there was some fixin' up needed before winter sets in.'

'It get pretty bad around here?' Ben wondered.

Ashburn nodded. 'One of the drawbacks. Big snows. And plenty of wind. Have to watch the herds mighty close. Seen them drift thirty, forty mile, if we don't keep on them. Sure makes it mean when we round-up.'

'How much acreage have you got, anyway?' Ben asked, surprised by what Ashburn had said.

'Own a hundred sections. Got another fifty thousand acres of free range I'm usin'.'

'Nobody on it?'

'Not now. Been two or three families try it.'

'You have to move them off?'

'Didn't need to. Land itself took care of them. This is good cow country, and nothin' else. Too much heat in the summer, too much bad weather in the winter. And it's a long way to water when the rain don't come.

'I try to tell them they can't make a go of farmin' out here but nobody ever listens. Got to find out for themselves. Worst thing is they break the ground, try to seed it. All they raise is a crop of dust, and that's bad for everybody.

'But I won't fight them. I figure every man's got a right to a piece of this country, same as I had. Only thing, if they'd listen to some of us that's been around for a spell, we could spare them a lot of sweat and heartbreak.'

Ben nodded. 'My pa always said the only kind of advice a man will listen to is the kind he wants to hear.'

'Sure the gospel truth,' Tom Ashburn agreed.

At noon they ate lunch in a small grove of trees where a spring trickled from a ledge of rock in a clear, cold stream. They had bacon and sliced beef sandwiches, prepared for them by the cook, and topped them off with slices of layer cake made by Sally. Ashburn brewed the coffee himself, maintaining no woman alive could boil up a cup strong enough to suit him.

Three hours later they caught up with the herd that was being moved to the western side of the range and paused there to have a few words with the riders who were handling the chore. It was Ben's first close look at Lazy A cattle and he could not help mentally comparing these fat, sleek animals to the lean, rangy brutes he had labored so hard to raise in the wilds of Mexico.

'Boys sure have took to you,' Tom Ashburn observed, when they were again moving on. He gave a sly look. 'It have anything to do with that swellin' on your lip and that bruise on your jaw?'

'Just a bit of a misunderstanding,' Jordan said, skirting the subject.

'A misunderstandin' with Oran Bishop at the bottom of it, I'll bet!' Ashburn snorted. 'Well he's goin' to be one of your problems, you can bank on it. A good boy but he just ain't ever growed up.'

'We'll get along,' Ben said. 'You have a winter range?'

The rancher shrugged. 'Not much difference in the land. Usually let cold weather catch the stock wherever it happens to be. You got some kind of a scheme?'

'Was wondering why it wouldn't be smart to put everything as far north as we can. Then when the snow hit, they'd just naturally drift south. Grass there would be in good shape then, and it might cut down on a lot of work when spring round-up comes.'

Ashburn wheeled to Sally. 'See what I was talkin' about? Man's either a natural cowman, or he ain't.' He swung back to Ben. 'That's smart thinkin'. You start doin' it—movin' all the stock north—soon as you're ready.'

'Maybe a little late now to do any good this year.'

'No, don't figure it is. Snow won't hit until late November, maybe even December. You can expect a couple of months yet of good weather.'

'Then we'll get at it tomorrow. Sooner we move that beef off the lower range, the faster the grass will come back.'

Ashburn murmured in satisfaction. Ben was aware of Sally's glance upon him, of the smile on her lips, and the pleasure in her eyes. She seemed as proud of his suggestion as her father had been—a suggestion that appeared no more than common sense to him.

And the north range, as far as they rode into it, was in excellent condition; indeed, it seemed hardly to have been worked. Ben doubted if there had been a steer on it for months.

'Settles it for sure,' Ashburn said. 'Comes when a man don't look after things himself. Crew gets lazy. Want to stay close to the bunkhouse so's they can ride in every night at dark. You change all that Ben. Keep them livin' in the line shacks, if you've a mind to. I'll back you all the way.'

The rancher paused, swept the land with a fond, remembering gaze. 'Place has been good to me,' he said. 'And I been worryin' some about it goin' to hell. Reckon I can forget that now and start sleepin' easy.' He shifted on his saddle, turned to Jordan and the girl. His face was calm, settled, reflecting the ease he felt.

'I'll be leavin' you here. Had enough of this blasted horse for one day. Sally, you take Ben on over to the brakes. Want him to see the bad part as well as the good... So long.'

Ashburn rode off abruptly, hunched

forward on his horse, a man turned weary by the years.

Sally and Ben continued on, making a wide circuit of the land, traveling along the edge of the wild, brushy area Ashburn had mentioned. Cattle were never permitted to graze in that section, Sally told him. Too many were lost in the brakes and it was always a temptation to rustlers.

When he had taken his look, they swung back to the south for the ranch. The afternoon sun was warm and they rode slowly, easily. After a time the girl spoke.

'You've seen it all, or most of it,' she said. 'Do you still think it's so fine?'

'The best,' he answered. 'Man can be proud of a spread like this.'

'It can also be a prison,' Sally said quietly. 'It has held my father here for thirty years. And I guess it will keep him until he dies.'

'Not much reason to leave it,' Jordan said. A rider silhouetting the horizon claimed his attention momentarily. 'Or do you think there is?' he finished.

The girl shrugged, her face turned from him as she looked toward the smokey hills far to the east.

'Sometimes I think so. Sometimes I wish I could go away, leave and never see this ranch again. I guess if I had been born a son instead of a daughter it would be different.' She hesitated, added, 'Do you plan ever to return to Mexico?'

The rider had disappeared. Ben was silent for several moments. 'Maybe. I don't know. My parents are buried there and the land, for what it is worth, is still mine. Way I feel now I want no more of the *Barranca Negra*.'

'I've never seen my father like this before,' Sally said quietly. 'I think he's found the son he's always wanted at last. He'll want you to stay here.'

Jordan glanced at her. 'And you?'

She moved her slim shoulders. Her face, profiled to him, was delicately molded, soft looking. 'I would like it, too,' she replied in complete honesty.

'Was told last night to keep my eyes off you.'

'That Oran Bishop!' she cried angrily. 'That sounds like him. He has no right—'

'I don't intend to pay any attention to him,' Ben said, and checked his words suddenly. The lone horseman had appeared again. He was still too distant to recognize but there was no doubt now in Ben Jordan's mind that he was deliberately maintaining his position and pace to coincide with theirs. It was as though he were keeping a close watch over them. It could mean nothing, or it could mean a great deal. Jordan decided there was no point in taking any chances.

'I think we'd better be getting back to the ranch,' he said, touching his horse with spurs.

Sally looked at him in surprise. 'Why?'

He grinned at her. 'Be suppertime,' he said, as they broke into a gallop.

It was full dark when they reached the lip of the swale and started down the long, gentle slope to the ranch. Lamplight glowed in the windows of the houses, warm and friendly. There had been no more sign of the mysterious, distant rider and the thought of that had faded from his mind.

He was thinking of how fine a life a man could make on a spread such as the Lazy A—with a wife like Sally, and wondered if he dared hope. It was possible, he decided, but before he could do anything he still had his promise to Woodward to fulfil. That could easily be discharged now.

'How far is it to Langford?' he asked.

She glanced at him curiously. 'Langford? About a day's ride north-east. Why?'

'Some business there I've got to attend to.'

'That's fine!' Sally exclaimed, pleased. 'I've been meaning to make the trip myself. There are somethings I need to buy. We can go together. When?'

'Soon as I can get the crew to working at what I want done.'

'Let's make it this week,' she said as they rode in to the yard. 'I would have gone today, but changed my mind.'

Jordan reached out, caught the pinto's

bridle, and halted him. Sally looked at him questioningly.

'Thanks for that,' Ben said.

She smiled at him. 'I enjoyed it, too,' she said and dropped from her saddle. She started across the yard but paused, 'Come on up to the house when you're ready. I'll have Mattie set out supper for you.'

'Be there in ten minutes,' Jordan replied and turned the horses over to the hostler.

He swung toward his cabin, whistling softly under his breath. As he rounded the feed barn, he pulled up sharply. A dark figure emerged from the rear window of his quarters, leaped to the ground, and raced for the deeper shadows along side.

'You!' Ben shouted, breaking into a run. 'Stop—or I'll shoot!'

But when he reached the corner of the structure the intruder had disappeared into the night. Jordan's face hardened. He had been right. The rider he had seen in the hills had not been there by accident but for a reason. Someone had wanted close tabs kept on him—someone who was interested in something inside the cabin. Sudden fear lifted within Ben Jordan as realization came to him. He spun, ran swiftly to the door.

CHAPTER ELEVEN

Even in the darkness Jordan could see the place was a shambles. Drawers had been pulled open, the bed stripped, furniture overturned; every conceivable nook that might conceal anything had been investigated. Ben glanced at the small rug he had pulled across the loose floor board. It appeared undisturbed.

Closing the door, and still in the dark, he dropped to his knees. Brushing the carpet aside, he lifted the plank. Relief flowed through him as his groping fingers felt the worn, smooth surface of leather, sought and touched the packets of currency and toyed with the gold coins. If it had been the money the intruder was looking for, he had failed to find it.

Jordan gave that consideration. It had to be the money, or, at least, the saddlebags, for he had brought nothing else with him when he rode into Ashburn's. And who would be so interested in what he was carrying in the leather pouches?

He replaced the floor board carefully and pulled the carpet and chair back into place. The saddlebags were the only thing anyone could be after; it was hardly possible that any of Ashburn's hired hands knew he was in possession of a small fortune. That added up to one answer: the trespasser was searching for something he did not know the exact nature of—an article he felt would have bearing on Jordan's presence.

That brought Ben's thoughts to a dead stop on Oran Bishop. He had been the only man to take note of the saddlebags, to remark on the jealous care with which Jordan accorded them. It would be Bishop then, possibly curious as to what made the pouches so valuable, and hopeful they would contain something with which he could discredit Ben in the eyes of Tom Ashburn. The rider in the hills, watching to be certain Jordan did not return unexpectedly early, could have been Oran's friend, Ross Colby. It was all an outside guess—but it made sense.

Suddenly angered, Ben left his cabin and walked the short distance to the bunkhouse. He pushed open the door and entered. Several of the punchers had already crawled into their bunks. Cruz Rodriguez and three others sat at a table playing poker for matches. They glanced up as Jordan halted before them. The Mexican smiled, sobered quickly when he saw Ben's face.

'*Que pasa, amigo?*'

'Who just came in here—during the last five minutes?'

The riders looked at each other. Rodriguez

said, 'Nobody. Who do you look for?'

Jordan shook his head. 'Not sure.' He moved deeper into the room, made a slow tour of the bunks. Bishop and Colby were among those absent. That would mean they were part of the crew nighthawking the cattle. He halted near the door.

'Any of you seen Oran, or Ross Colby since you rode in?'

'They come to the herd at dark,' Rodriguez said. 'We leave to eat. They stay. I have not seen them since.'

That had little meaning. The two men could have slipped away unnoticed. One of the punchers started to rise.

'You want them, Mr Jordan? Be right pleased to go get them for you.'

Ben said, 'No, let it go. I'll see them in the morning. Good night.'

He left the bunkhouse but halted when he reached the yard. All was quiet and for a time he stood there, his shoulders squared against the night sky while he lost himself in thought. One thing came through to him quick and clear; he must get Walt Woodward's money off his hands. It was dangerous to have it around any longer.

He wheeled, headed for the main house where a lamp still burned in the kitchen. He would tell Ashburn he needed to make a trip into Langford that next morning. He would get it done at once.

But Tom Ashburn had already gone to bed, as had Sally. Jordan ate his meal of cold, sliced beef, warmed over biscuits and coffee in solitude, deciding he would talk to the rancher first thing that following morning. And it was probably best that he not take Sally with him. He was only assuming the intruder who had searched his quarters had been Oran Bishop. There could be another, someone who had learned he had the money, somebody besides Bart Crawford and his outlaw friends who was out to get the twenty thousand dollars he had sworn to deliver to Olivia Woodward. There could be danger.

He finished his supper and walked back into the yard. Far from sleep, he strolled on to the barn, looked in briefly at the sorrel contentedly crunching his ration of grain in one of the stalls, and then, keeping to the shadows, circled the yard to its opposite side where he could stand in the brushy windbreak planted years ago by Ashburn. There, unseen, he could watch his cabin. The intruder might pay a return visit, Ben reasoned, if he thought no one was around.

The night was cool and quiet. Off to the east a coyote barked and fell silent. An owl swished across the yard on motionless wings, and then came to a halt somewhere beyond the cook's vegetable garden. Inside the bunkhouse someone laughed and Cruz

Rodriguez said something in quick Spanish. The light in the kitchen winked out as Mattie, the cook, wound up her chores and went off to bed.

A faint breeze began to stir, drifting in from the west, fresh with the scent of grass and juniper, almost sharp with a breath of winter. Jordan glanced to the sky, a vast, black arch studded with low hanging, glittering stars. A cold sky, he thought, and snow could not be too far off. It would come sooner than Tom Ashburn had predicted. He must get the crew busy and prepare for the days when the weather would turn bad and neither man nor beast would find it possible to move about.

Tomorrow. He would start the crew gathering the herds that next morning, get them moving north to fresh grass—His thoughts halted. He would not be there. He must make the trip into Langford and rid himself of the responsibility that lay so heavily on his shoulders. It would take two days, even more if he had trouble locating Ollie Woodward. He could arrive there and find her out of town, or possibly moved away.

Yet if he were to fulfill his new obligations to Tom Ashburn, he could not afford to waste even one day.

He stepped from the windbreak of tamarisk, and crossed to the bunkhouse. The card game had broken up and now Cruz Rodriguez squatted on his heels, back pressed against the wall of the building as he smoked a final cigarette. He looked up and grinned, as Jordan approached.

'You find sleep comes hard, *señor*,' he said, stating it as a fact rather than a question. 'Perhaps it is because the *Barranca Negra* teaches a man always to keep one eye open for death.'

'Down there, if a man is not careful, it comes too soon,' Jordan agreed.

'But there are other things that trouble you, no?'

Ben nodded. 'Got to make a trip to Langford. Be gone a couple of days, maybe more. I want all the stock moved onto the north range. Like to have the crew get at it in the morning. Want you to pass the word along.'

Rodriguez stared at the glowing tip of his cigarette. He placed it between his lips, inhaled, and then exhaled a cloud of smoke. 'Up here, *amigo*,' he said quietly, 'one such as I—a Mexican—does not give an order.'

Ben stirred impatiently. 'It's my order, not yours. I'm only asking you to repeat it since I won't be here myself.'

Rodriguez flipped the cigarette into the yard. 'It shall be as you wish. I will repeat the order.'

'If anybody balks, tell them they'll answer

to me when I get back. Main thing is I want the stock grazing up there before bad weather hits so the rest of the range gets a chance to shape up for winter.'

Rodriguez said, 'I understand, *señor*. This journey you must take to Langford—it is important.'

'Has to be done,' Jordan replied. 'No way out of it.'

'The *patron*—Ashburn, he knows of this?'

'I figure on telling him in the morning.'

The Mexican was silent for a long time. Then, 'And you will return, *amigo*? He is a fine man and he thinks much of you. I would not like to see him sad.'

'I'll be back, Cruz. Depend on it.'

'It is enough,' Rodriguez said, thrusting out his hand. '*Adios. Buena suerte.*'

'*Adios*, and thanks,' Ben said enclosing the man's fingers in his own. He turned then, walked to his quarters.

Not bothering to remove his clothing, Jordan stretched out on the bed, his pistol placed nearby for instant use should the intruder return again. Sleep came quickly to him now that the decision to deliver Woodward's money had been made.

He awoke at the first gray streaks of dawn. Washing himself from the bowl and pitcher on the dresser, he made himself ready to travel. That done he paused in the center of the room to formulate a plan. He would first have his breakfast and tell Tom Ashburn of his need to go to Langford. Then he would return to his quarters, take the saddlebags from their place of concealment, get the sorrel and leave. It could be done with a minimum of waste motion and time—unless he had trouble with Sally.

But there was a possibility she would not be there for the early meal. She had been tired; she could sleep late.

He stepped to the door, pulled it open—and came to a quick stop. Four riders were pulling into the hitchrack in front of Ashburn's house. Four grim, dusty men. He knew them all—Crawford, Aaron, Gates, and Arlie Davis.

CHAPTER TWELVE

Ben Jordan withdrew into the room quickly and closed the door. The outlaws again! He had thought they were off his trail, and that he had lost them for good. How could they have tracked him to Ashburn's? In those tight, frustrating moments, he searched his mind for an answer.

Tuck—one of Slaughter's men! They had been talking... He had mentioned that he was headed north to take a job on the Lazy A. Crawford must have questioned all of the trail herd crew.

Jordan swore angrily. This changed everything. Of course, he could talk to Tom Ashburn, and call upon him for help. And the Lazy A hands would likely stand by him in a showdown. But as it had been with Slaughter, Jordan was reluctant to involve others in his own trouble; a man skinned his own cats and looked for no one else to give him a hand.

He wheeled to the cache where he had hidden the money. There was only one thing he could do now—leave, get off the Lazy A before the outlaws saw him.

Throwing the saddlebags over his shoulder, he let himself out the rear window, hurried across the open ground to the barn. The hostler was nowhere in sight and Ben threw his gear onto the sorrel in quick, practiced motions. Mounting, he rode through the wide doorway, dropped back behind the bulky structure and circled the ranch, keeping the tamarisk windbreak between the buildings and him. When he reached the end of the dense, feathery growth he halted. The ranch, clearly visible, lay below him.

Crawford who had come off the black, stood now, one foot on the porch of Ashburn's house while he talked to the rancher. Near the door Ben could see both Sally and her mother. Three of the hired hands, one of them Oran Bishop, were coming around the side from the dining hall, apparently curious as to the purpose of the four strangers.

They would not be long discovering that he had fled, Ben realized, and immediately pulled off below the crest of the rise and struck northward at a good lope. It would be wise to put as much distance as possible between him and the Lazy A within the next half hour.

He pressed the gelding hard for the first ten miles and then, topping out a high ridge, he looked back. There were no riders in sight. A sigh of relief slipped from his lips. If luck were with him, there would be doubt as to where he was; they might think he was somewhere on the range with the herd, since no one had seen his departure. If it worked that way the outlaws would lose several hours—ample time for him to reach the town of Langford and rid himself of the money.

He saw the settlement, three dozen or so graying shacks and buildings, huddled in the center of a brushy swale, shortly after noon. The gelding had made surprisingly good time, eating up the miles with his tireless, long legs and easy stride. Pleased that the journey had been much shorter than he had anticipated, Jordan rode on the crest of the hill where he had paused, and then started down the final two mile stretch of lane that led into the town. If all went well he should be able to turn back for Ashburn's place before dark, that very day.

He reached the bottom of the slope, the half way point, passed one or two run-down shacks, once homes of squatters but now deserted, and loped on. He would go first to the general store; storekeepers always knew where everyone lived and could tell him where to locate Ollie Woodward.

Unexpectedly the sorrel checked his run and slid to a halt. The big red horse reared, startled by the sudden appearance of three riders who burst from the depths of the dense brush that lined the road.

Ben Jordan's hand dropped instinctively to the pistol at his hip, and fell slowly away as he looked into the muzzles of the guns held by the trio. One, a husky, dark man, with a somewhat better appearance than the others, pushed out ahead.

'Forget you've got that hogleg,' he said, moving in close. He studied Jordan for several moments. Then, 'Where'd you get that horse?'

Anger whipped through Ben, not only at being accosted in so highhanded a manner, but at his own carelessness. Just as the end of his problem was in sight, he had allowed himself to get tripped up.

'Not that it's any of your business,' he snapped, 'he was given to me.'

'I'm makin' it my business,' the dark faced man said. He reached into his pocket, produced a star. 'Name's Sharpe. Deputy town marshal.' He waved his hand at the pair behind him. 'Frick and Rosen. They're workin' with me. We've been on the lookout for that sorrel. What's your name, mister?'

Jordan breathed easier. 'Ben Jordan—and I can explain about the horse. Belonged to a man named Woodward, Walt Woodward.'

'I know him,' Sharpe said.

'He got shot up. I found him dying in a shack, back in the hills. I'd lost my horse so he gave me his.'

'Why?' Sharpe's tone was cool, suspicious.

'I just told you—and I agreed to do him a favor.'

'Favor?' Sharpe repeated, his voice lifting. Frick and Rosen moved up beside him, rifles still cocked and leveled at Jordan's breast.

'Something personal,' Ben said.

The lawman studied Jordan in suspicious silence. Finally he said, 'Maybe you could have killed him, stolen the sorrel.'

'No,' Ben rapped impatiently, realizing in that same moment that he had no proof of any sort, except the twenty thousand dollars. 'It's just the way I've said it.'

Sharpe rode forward, lifted Jordan's gun from its holster, thrust it into his own belt. He leaned to the side, elbow on the horn of his saddle. 'This favor you're talkin' about, what was it?'

Jordan hesitated, and then shrugged. Telling the whole story would likely be the only way he could prove his innocence. A man, killing another for his horse, would not be delivering a small fortune in cash to the widow. And he was talking to the law; there could be no danger.

'Asked me to carry some money to his wife—widow. He'd just sold out a ranch, he said. Made me promise to see she got the cash.'

'Twenty thousand dollars,' Sharpe said.

Ben stared. 'How'd you know that?'

Sharpe shook his head. 'Woodwards are friends of mine. Personal friends. Knew about the deal from the start.' He paused, cast a sidewards glance at Frick and Rosen. 'We've been worryin' about Walt. The money in those saddlebags?'

Jordan nodded. 'Be obliged if you'd take me to Mrs Woodward. Want to get it off my hands.'

'No use you havin' to bother about it any longer,' the lawman said. 'I'll see she gets it.'

'Appreciate that, too, but I'll have to do it personally. Gave my word to Woodward.'

'We'll do it my way,' Sharpe said quietly and firmly. He motioned to Frick. 'Tubo, get the saddlebags.'

'Now, hold up a minute!' Ben said. 'Don't see where it makes any difference to you—'

'You walk easy, mister!' the lawman cut in sharply. 'I'm still not sure I swallow that yarn you handed us about findin' Woodward dyin', and him givin' you his horse.'

'Then what the hell am I doing here bringing his widow all that money?' Jordan shouted, furious. 'If I had killed Woodward and stolen his horse, I'd be going the other way fast as I could!'

'Point in your favor,' Sharpe said calmly. 'I'll tell it to the marshal. Get the saddlebags, Tubo.'

Jordan sat motionless, helpless, as Frick pulled the pouches free and handed them to Sharpe. The deputy unbuckled one side, checked the money. He nodded as if satisfied.

'All here, far as I can tell,' he said. He turned to Rosen. 'Barney, take Jordan here in and lock him up until we get things cleared around. Want to talk to Mrs Woodward about it, see what she thinks.'

Jordan sighed in disgust. 'You're wasting a lot of time, time I sure don't have to spare, deputy. I can't afford to lay around in jail for two or three days. I've got a job to get back to.'

Sharpe considered that for several moments. Then, 'Reckon you're right,' he said. 'Won't keep you waitin' any longer than I just have to. And you give me your word you'll hang around until I straighten this out and I won't lock you up. Just you check in at the hotel. Guess the word of a man honest enough to ride clear across the territory with another man's money, ought to be reliable.'

'Sure ought,' Barney Rosen agreed.

'Won't take no longer'n tomorrow mornin'. Main thing is for me to explain it all to Pogue—he's the marshal. And I've got to see what Mrs Woodward wants to do about that horse.'

'Her husband gave him to me.'

'Know that. You told us. But you'll need a bill of sale. Woodward was pretty well known around here and people will be recognizing that sorrel of his. You'd better have some papers proving he's yours, or you're liable to get strung up for horse stealing.'

Ben shifted on the saddle. No matter what his personal thoughts were, it seemed he had no choice but to do as the deputy directed. 'All right,' he said. 'I'll be at the hotel. But hurry things along. I want to be on my way home by morning.'

'We'll sure move fast as we can,' Sharpe said. 'Hotel's down at the end of the street. I'll go first off and see Mrs Woodward.' He reached down, plucked Jordan's gun from his belt and returned it.

'Might as well have this back,' he said, and started to move off. He drew up suddenly.

'One thing more, don't think you ought to mention anything about this money to anybody. Risky business having twenty thousand dollars just layin' around. Sure wouldn't want anything to happen to it before the widow Woodward could get it stashed away in the bank.'

Jordan said, 'All right, deputy. Whatever you say,' and rode on toward a scattering of buildings.

CHAPTER THIRTEEN

Jordan entertained no thoughts of registering into Langford's hotel. He would allow the deputy until nightfall to satisfy himself that all was honest-and-above-board and then, whether Sharpe liked it or not, he was returning to the Lazy A. If there were matters still to be cleared up the lawman could come to him at Ashburn's. He felt he had fulfilled his promise to Walt Woodward—at least he had done so to all practical purposes—and that ended it.

He angled the sorrel into a hitchrack in front of a restaurant, the only one in the settlement, it appeared, and dismounted. He had eaten no breakfast and now hunger was making itself known. The café was far from clean but he settled down at the counter and ordered himself a meal.

It was good to have the responsibility of Woodward's money off his hands, and with it the knowledge that Bart Crawford and his men would not again be dogging his trail. Yet there was something about the whole affair that left him vaguely dissatisfied and disturbed. He was not feeling the tremendous relief that he had imagined would be his, once the chore was finished; instead there was a gnawing discontent, a sense of having left a job partly undone.

But there had been no other way. Sharpe was a lawman, a deputy marshal according to what he had said, as well as the badge he carried, and he had claimed to be a close friend of the Woodwards. The fact he knew the exact amount of money in the saddlebags further verified that statement.

Still ... He wished now he had insisted more forcefully on delivering the money himself to Ollie Woodward. Sharpe and his two helpers could have accompanied him, if there were doubts in their minds as to his intentions. Ben stirred restlessly; that was the way he should have handled it.

His food came and he dallied and toyed with it for a full half hour, taking no pleasure from it. When he had had enough, he arose, paid his check and returned to the street. On the opposite side, a few doors down, he saw the marshal's office and jail. Leading the sorrel, he crossed over.

The lawman's headquarters were empty, the single cell vacant. Ben turned, walked back into the open. A man standing in front of a saloon a short distance farther on, looked at him inquiringly.

'You huntin' for Marshal Pogue?'

Jordan said, 'Yes. Any idea where I can find him?'

'Nope. Sure don't. But I reckon he's around somewheres. Might be he's out in the country.'

The dissatisfaction within Ben Jordan continued to grow. 'What's his deputy's name?'

'Ain't got no regular man. Once in a while appoints himself a special deputy when they's somethin' that's got to be done like movin' pris'ners.'

'Know one called Sharpe?'

The man thought for a moment, shrugged. 'Don't recollect the name, but could be. Like I said he hires on somebody now and then. What's the trouble? You needin' help?'

Jordan gave him no reply. After a time he said, 'How about Mrs Olivia Woodward—know where she lives?'

'Ollie? Sure,' the man grinned broadly, 'down to the end of the street, turn left. Green house settin' off to itself.'

'Thanks,' Ben said and swung onto the sorrel.

Jordan found the Woodward home with no difficulty. He tied the gelding to a fence post, made his way along a path to the door and knocked. There was no immediate answer and after a time he repeated the summons.

The panel opened. A heavy-eyed woman, her face smeared with cosmetics she had not troubled to remove the previous night, straw-colored hair falling in disarray about her shoulders, and clad in a faded robe which she clutched at the neck, stared out at him. Once she had possessed beauty but it was gone now, replaced by that brassy hardness common to saloon women.

'What do you want?' she demanded harshly.

'You Mrs Woodward—Olivia Woodward?'

'That's me,' she said. 'Who are you?'

'I knew your husband,' Ben said. 'Name is Jordan.'

He watched Ollie Woodward's haggard face for some reaction. If the deputy had been there, had delivered the money to her, she would recognize his name as that of the man who had brought it. Her features remained stolid.

'Come on in,' she said, retreating into the shaded, over-furnished room. 'Where is Walt?'

Jordan, pushed by his own fears, entered.

'There been three men here to see you, one of them Sharpe, the deputy marshal?'

Ollie Woodward's eyes narrowed slightly. 'Sharpe, the deputy?' she repeated as though startled. 'No. Why would he be coming here?'

'You know him?'

'Yes, I know him.'

Jordan took a deep breath. 'He's bringing you the money your husband sent you. Twenty thousand dollars.' Ben paused, 'I've got bad news, Mrs Woodward. Walt's dead.'

The woman stared. 'Dead? You sure?'

'Was with him when it happened. Outlaws shot him. I buried him myself. Before he died he made me promise to deliver the money he got from the sale of your ranch to you. Twenty thousand dollars, he said it was.'

'You say Al Sharpe has it now?'

Jordan nodded. 'They—Sharpe and a couple of men he called Frick and Rosen—stopped me at the edge of town. Thought I'd stolen your husband's horse. When I explained what I was doing Sharpe took over the money, said he was a personal friend of yours and he'd take it to you. Told me I'd have to wait around until he cleared up things. He a friend of the family?'

'Yes, for a long time.'

'Said he'd bring the money straight to you. I've been dodging outlaws all the way across the territory to keep my promise to your husband. Wish now I hadn't turned it over to Sharpe.'

Ollie Woodward smiled. 'It will be all right,' she said. 'I'll get it. Al must have gotten side-tracked on the way. When did you say you gave it to him?'

'About an hour ago.'

She rose, moved to the door and opened it for him. 'Want to thank you for all the trouble you went through, Mr Jordan. And don't worry about your promise to Walt. You've kept it.'

'Wish I could make myself feel that way,' Ben replied, moving into the open. 'But if you're satisfied, I guess I should be. What about the horse?'

'Horse?'

'The sorrel. Walt gave him to me but I've got no papers to prove he's mine. The deputy said I had better get a bill of sale from you.'

'Of course, and I want you to have him. Tell you what, the least I can do for you in return, is cook you a good supper before you leave. You get your bill of sale made up and be back here about dark. I'll sign it, then we'll eat.'

'Sounds fine, but you don't need to go to all that trouble—'

'No trouble. You do what I say. Risking your life to bring that money—a good supper will be little enough pay.'

Jordan walked on into the yard. 'See you at dark, then,' he said, smiling, and continued on to where the sorrel waited.

It was all finished now. He could stop stewing about it. Ollie Woodward, while seemingly not particularly saddened by her husband's death, had exhibited no alarm when she learned that Deputy Sharpe was in possession of her money and had failed so far to deliver it. But she was right, of course; he could have been delayed for some cause. And he guessed he was pressing things too hard. It had actually been little more than an hour since Sharpe had relieved him of the saddlebags.

He was pleased that the sorrel was to become his legally. Now he need fear no subsequent problems in that matter. He would go to a livery stable, obtain a blank bill of sale and fill in a description of the horse. With Ollie Woodward's signature properly affixed, the transfer would be above question.

He mounted, turned back up the lane, heading for Langford's one street. He had three or four hours to kill before dark and the hour at which he was to return to Olivia Woodward's. The smart thing would be to go somewhere, get a little sleep, if he intended to spend the night riding back to the Lazy A. The livery stable where he planned to get a bill of sale—he could crawl into the loft and take a short nap on the hay...

He reached the corner, halted, his eyes searching for such an establishment. He stiffened suddenly. Five men, riding abreast, turned into the far end of the street and came slowly, purposefully onward. Crawford and his friends again ... and with them was Oran Bishop.

CHAPTER FOURTEEN

A smile cracked Ben Jordan's lips as he watched the grim-faced outlaws approach. The laugh was on them now. The money was safe where they could not touch it. They were too late. And then Jordan frowned. What was Bishop doing with them? There was no denying the ill-feeling that existed between him and the puncher, but he did not think Oran so bitter that he would seek to gratify it by siding in with outlaws such as Bart Crawford.

Drawing back until the corner of the building where he had halted shielded him from the men's view, he watched as the riders moved along the street and came to a stop in its center. Several persons emerged from the doorways of the weathered stores and stared at them curiously. There appeared to be a discussion between the five, something that had to do with the marshal, for all glanced now and then towards the lawman's office.

Jordan contemplated riding out into the open, moving up to them and having his moment of victory, but the presence of Oran Bishop among the group held him back. He could find no logical reason for the blond puncher's being with them unless—Jordan's thoughts came to a halt—unless Crawford actually was a lawman, as he had claimed to be at Slaughter's camp. And if that were true then Walt Woodward, far from being an honest rancher, had been an outlaw in possession of stolen money!

The possibility of that struck Ben forcibly, pinning him motionless to his saddle. It could be true; and it would account for Oran Bishop's presence. When he looked back over the past days' incidents, recalled the words spoken by Woodward, Crawford's actions, the way Ollie Woodward, far from a grieving wife, had received the news, a pattern began to fall into place.

But if it were so—Woodward an outlaw and Crawford a sheriff or marshal—he was now little better off in the eyes of the lawman than before. Crawford would never believe his story of handing over the saddlebags and the twenty thousand dollars to Al Sharpe; he would have to have proof in the form of the deputy himself. He must go—

A door slammed somewhere behind Jordan. He half turned, glanced down the narrow lane. Ollie Woodward, carrying a small carpetbag, was coming from her house, walking hurriedly. She was fully dressed with a light coat thrown over her arm. She cut sharp right when she left her yard, headed not for the street and the business section of Langford, but for the dense, wooded area that lay east of the town.

As Ben Jordan watched her, his convictions grew. Ollie Woodward was leaving hastily. She was avoiding the settlement. That she had no intention of meeting him at dark was also perfectly clear; such had been only a means for getting rid of him. It all meant something—something that concerned him vitally.

Jordan wheeled the sorrel about. As the gelding swung around, he moved briefly into the street. Ben flung a glance toward the five men and saw they had seen him. Crawford's hand came up swiftly. There was sharp glint of sunlight on metal and then a gunshot echoed along the buildings. Ben felt the warm breath of the bullet and saw the five riders break into a charging run.

He drove his spurs into the gelding, sent him plunging down the lane. He swung off to the right of Woodward's place, drove hard for the trees and underbrush beyond it. He did not want to rush on after Ollie Woodward—not yet. He would lead Crawford and his party off to the side, lose them, and double back. She would not go far.

The sorrel thundered along a hedge of wild roses, sailing effortlessly over a low, sagging fence and gained the thicker growth. At that moment Crawford and his followers rounded the corner. Jordan, low in the saddle, did not look back. He heard Bishop's voice yelling something at him but the words were lost in the pounding of the gelding's hoofs. He expected Crawford to open up again with his pistol, but no more shots came.

He raced straight ahead through the welter of rocks, brush and scrubby trees for several hundred yards. Now there was no need to look over his shoulder; he could tell his pursuers were coming on from the hammering of their horses, and he knew they were not far behind. But they were having difficulty keeping him in sight. As they cleared the fence he heard Crawford's shout.

'Keep bearin' right! He's headin' that way!'

Jordan grinned and began to curve the sorrel to the left. The brush was dragging at him, tearing at his legs but it was screening his flight effectively. He pressed on letting the gelding have his head and pick his own way. Through the trees he began to see open ground, realizing they were coming into the open again.

He angled the big horse more sharply to the left, and was now riding in the exact opposite direction to that he had taken at the beginning. He listened for sounds of Crawford and the others, but could hear nothing. Evidently they were hanging to the course they had chosen at the start and still believed him to be somewhere ahead.

He broke out onto cleared ground suddenly and saw that he was on the lane that fronted the Woodward house. He pulled the sorrel to a stop and looked about. He was several hundred yards below the house—and below the point where he had last seen the woman. He cut around, sent the gelding up the lane at a trot, his glance searching through the brush for some signs of her.

When he came to a fork where a second lane angled off, he halted again. He dropped from the saddle and made a close inspection of the loose dust. The narrow, pointed toe imprints of a woman's foot were unmistakable. Jordan went back onto the gelding and headed him down the off-shooting side lane. He held the horse to a quiet walk. Ollie Woodward could not have gotten far.

He had no difficulty in following her.

Every few yards the print of her small foot was visible, and he knew he had only to use care to catch up eventually with her. Just what it would mean when he did, he had no idea, but that it all tied in with Sharpe and the money, he was certain.

Stolen money—and he had aided an outlaw in the furtherance of his crime. That he was an innocent party in the scheme was beside the point; the law would make no allowances for his actions unless, of course, he could recover the money and hand it over to the authorities. Only then might they be inclined to listen.

The money—twenty thousand dollars in gold coin and currency—where was it? He had last seen it when Al Sharpe, the deputy, had taken it from him, stating that he would take it to Ollie Woodward. The delivery had never been made, and now, here he was, Jordan thought, blindly following the woman for no good reason other than on a hunch that she was more involved than she purported to be, and would lead him to it. If the hunch didn't pan out ... Jordan brushed the possibility from his mind. He would ford that creek when he came to it.

The area was becoming more overgrown, the lane less clearly cut. They were somewhere east of the settlement, he reckoned, in a section that was seldom visited by the residents. A few moments later he caught his first glimpse of Ollie.

She was still walking fast, the coat in one hand, the small bag in the other. Jordan halted, allowed her to get well ahead again. He did not want her looking over her shoulder and seeing him on her trail. But she seemed in much too great a hurry for that. She was bent on reaching some particular place—or meeting some person, as quickly as possible.

Ben thought he heard sounds of Crawford and his men shortly after that and he continued to wait and listen in the warm hush. The noise came from the direction where he had last seen the five riders and he wondered if they had discovered their error and had turned back and were now combing through the brush for him.

In all likelihood this was the case. The trees and rocks ended a short distance to the south, just as they had to the east. The grove had appeared to be a sort of oasis in the center of which Langford had sprung up.

He heard nothing more and put the sorrel into motion once again. He covered a hundred yards, rounded a sharp turn in the lane—and found it empty for a considerable distance. Ollie Woodward had disappeared.

He glanced around hurriedly. She could have done nothing other than turn off. In that next moment he saw her again, a brief flash of color through the trees to his left.

She was walking up a narrow path toward a cabin that was set deep in the tangled brush. As Ben watched she reached the door, lifted the latch, and without hesitation, entered.

Jordan wheeled off the lane and quietly made his way to a point fifty yards or so from the weathered shack. Tying the sorrel securely to a clump of juniper, he worked in to the rear of the structure. There was but one small window, low off the ground. He dropped to his hands and knees, crept to the opening. Voices, laughter and conversation reached him.

Removing his hat, he raised himself carefully, quietly to where he could look in. The first face he saw was that of Al Sharpe.

CHAPTER FIFTEEN

Sharpe said, 'Always figured I'd make a dang good lawman! Got that square look!'

Everyone laughed. Jordan's body tensed. Sharpe was no deputy—he was an outlaw, too! And so were Frick and Barney Rosen. He had been wrong all the way. He shifted to where he had a better view of the cabin's interior.

Ollie Woodward sat on the edge of a cot upon which the saddlebags had been laid. The pouches were open and the money was partially visible. Sharpe leaned against a crudely built table, a bottle in his hand. Squatted on their heels, backs pressed against a wall were Rosen and Frick.

'Well, you sure was right,' Frick said, fumbling with his cigarette makings. 'You kept sayin' if we watched that road long enough old Walt'd show up. He didn't, but the money sure did.'

Sharpe nodded, took a drink from the bottle and handed it to Rosen. 'When I saw him line out that night after we robbed the bank, I knew he was bad hit. I aimed to follow and then some of that damned posse got on my tail, and I lost him. Didn't worry me none, however. I figured he'd come waggin' back to Ollie sooner or later. Or, if he couldn't make it, he'd be sucker enough to send the money to her somehow.'

Ollie Woodward turned to Sharpe. 'That's why you've been playing the good family friend so much here lately. You were keeping an eye on me.'

'Man looks after his own interests,' Sharpe said.

She nodded. 'I still come in for my share—Walt's share, don't I, Al?'

Sharpe grinned. 'I got a better idea. Two shares make one big one. Why don't you and me tie up? Won't have to be worryin' about Walt now. Could have ourselves quite a time with ten thousand dollars.'

Ollie Woodward shrugged. 'Sure, why not?'

Sharpe studied her for several moments. 'Never could figure what you seen in Walt. He sure wasn't your kind.'

'He was good to me,' the woman said tiredly. 'And he usually had some money.'

'We'll have plenty of that from now on,' Sharpe said. 'And when this runs out, the boy's and me'll find us another hick town bank to bust open.'

The woman looked down. 'And you'll die out in the brush somewhere, just like Walt did, some day. I had a feeling the night you came over to the house and planned it all out—a feeling that something bad was going to happen—'

'None of that now!' Sharpe broke in. 'You're soundin' like a wife already and I won't have it!'

Ollie moved her shoulders in a faint gesture of resignation. She extended her hand to Rosen for the whiskey bottle. She took a swallow, shuddered, passed it on to Tubo Frick.

'I'll never learn to like that stuff,' she murmured. 'When do we leave, Al?'

'Soon as it's dark.'

'I don't think we ought to wait that long.'

'Why not? We sure don't want nobody seein' us leavin' the country.'

'That cowboy, Jordan, that brought the

money. He was pretty upset when he found out you hadn't given it to me. I think I smoothed it over but he still might go to the marshal, and start asking questions.'

'Let him,' Sharpe said. 'And if he comes around again, tell him you've got it—the money your lovin' husband sent you for sellin' his ranch.'

Sharpe began to laugh, unable to continue. Frick and Rosen joined in but Ollie Woodward only smiled.

'Old Walt sure must've give him a yarn! And makin' him promise to tote all that money to his poor little wife, come hell or high water! Lord, what a sucker!'

Ben Jordan felt his face begin to burn. He had been a sucker, a greenhorn from the word go! Woodward had really taken him in.

'He's an honest man,' Ollie said in a quiet voice. 'Something we've all forgot how to be.'

'No difference,' Rosen observed drily. 'A sucker and an honest man, all the same thing.'

'Maybe Walt wasn't playing him for a sucker so much as he was interested in getting the money to us, so I could have his share,' the woman said. 'I'd like to think that's the way it was. And it could be.'

'Sure, sure,' Sharpe said impatiently. 'But Walt's dead, gone, buried. He done us a favor, gettin' the cash to us after he got shot up and knew he wasn't goin' to make it. That's fine, but forget about it and him. Does no good to keep hashin' over the dead.'

'I'm for that,' Rosen said, wagging his head. 'Gives a man the creeps...'

Sharpe reached down, picked up a packet of the currency. He rifled the edges thoughtfully. 'Maybe you ought to go back to your house,' he said, settling his attention on the woman. 'Just in case that greenhorn does take Pogue over to see you. We'll swing by when it's time and pick you up.'

Distrust was frank on Ollie Woodward's features. 'No, I'll stay here. I think we ought to leave now, but if you don't, all right, we'll wait.'

Sharpe laughed. 'Afraid we might forget to come by?'

Ollie said, 'Yes,' in a bold, candid way.

Sharpe roared with laughter. 'That's right, girl! Don't trust nobody. Look out for yourself!'

'What we goin' to do about eatin'?' Frick asked. 'Barney ain't got nothin' here in his shack. You reckon it's safe for one of us to go into town?'

'No,' Sharpe answered. 'Might run into that Jordan. He's still waitin' for me to tell him he can pull out.'

'How about Ollie then? Nobody'd pay any mind to her.'

'I'm not leaving here,' the woman said

stubbornly. 'If you want some food, one of you run over to my place and help yourself. You're not likely to bump into that cowboy there. He wasn't coming back until dark.'

'Comin' to your house?'

'For supper. Wanted me to sign some papers giving him Walt's horse.'

'A horse,' Frick said. 'We'll be needin' one for Ollie. Where'll we get one?'

Sharpe thought for a moment. 'Guess I should have grabbed Walt's sorrel when I had the chance. You know people around here, Barney; where can we get a nag for her?'

'Rancher about ten mile east of here. Reckon we can get one from him.'

'Settles that. Ollie can ride double with me until we get there. We'll figure to eat and get ourselves some grub from that rancher, too.'

Ben pulled back from the window, crouched low in the brush. He had all the answers now, but the problem that faced him was how to recover the money and capture the outlaws. Once accomplished he could turn them and the saddlebags over to Marshal Pogue—or to Bart Crawford; it didn't matter whom.

He considered the advisability of moving in on the men, but the odds were too long. It would be his one gun against three desperate outlaws, plus possibly, Ollie Woodward, who showed every sign of being as coolly efficient as they were. And the arrangement of the cabin would double his problem. After a moment he discarded the idea. He could not afford to make a mistake now; already he had allowed himself to be made a fool. This time he must be sure.

Pogue—the town marshal. There was the solution. Sharpe and the others planned to stay in the shack until dark. There would be plenty of time to ride to Langford, locate the lawman, recruit a posse and return.

But why go that far?

Why not call on Bart Crawford and his deputies? To allow him and his men to make the capture would undoubtedly ease some of the hard feeling that existed between the lawmen and himself. And they were somewhere close by.

On his hands and knees Ben started back for the gelding. He could hear Al Sharpe off on another tale of some sort, one that was providing much laughter for Tubo Frick and Barney Rosen. He could not hear Ollie Woodward's voice. Apparently she was not finding Al Sharpe's words amusing. That the widow had little use for the companions of her late husband was evident; that she was determined to have her share of the stolen money was also clear.

Still low, Jordan reached the stand of thick growth where he had hidden the sorrel. He was on the verge of rising when Bart

Crawford's voice, in a hoarse whisper, and coming from only a few steps ahead, halted him.

'His horse, all right. Means he's around close. Now, I want him—any way you can get him—dead or alive.'

CHAPTER SIXTEEN

Bart Crawford's grim words hammered at Jordan's brain: *dead or alive!* They were giving him no chance at all, no opportunity to prove his innocence. Crawford had determined only that the chase would end there. The corners of Ben Jordan's mouth hardened, a whiteness began to show along the edge of his jaw as anger swept through him.

Dead or alive—he would have something to say about that! Sure, he had let both Walt Woodward and Al Sharpe make a fool of him, but now he was in a position to rectify his mistakes. And whether Crawford and his men liked it or not, they were going to help him do it.

He raised himself cautiously. Crawford was off his horse, stood only a few paces away. He was facing the opposite way, having his close look at the sorrel's gear, apparently hopeful of finding the stolen money hidden about the saddle. Beyond him, still mounted, were Aaron, Gates, Davis and Oran Bishop.

Jordan drew his pistol. He would have to move fast. The instant he stepped from the brush he would reveal himself to the four riders. Everything depended on him reaching Crawford, jamming his gun into the man's back and forcing the others to hold their fire.

'What about that cabin over yonder?' Gates said. 'Could be he's holed up in there.'

'And leave his horse standin' out here like this?' Crawford answered, his tone derisive. 'No, he won't be doin' that. Place don't look much like anybody's been near it for years.'

'Still figure we ought to look.'

Ben Jordan, like a dark, shifting shadow, moved from the depths of the brush suddenly. In three strides he was crowding in behind Crawford and had his revolver digging into the man's spine.

'Hey—look out!' Gates exclaimed, startled. His hand swept downward for the weapon at his hip.

The others stared and then came to life. Jordan's sharp words froze them on the saddle.

'Don't try anything—not unless you want me to blow his guts out!'

Crawford, swearing in a deep angry voice, slowly raised his hands. Ben reached forward, pulled the lawman's weapon from its holster and thrust it into his own belt.

'Keep looking in that direction,' he ordered. 'I've got some talking to do.'

Crawford only grunted. Oran Bishop, his face red, his eyes snapping, said, 'You damned owlhoot! Knew there was something wrong the moment you rode into Ashburn's. You ought to be right pleased with yourself, fooling that old man like you did.'

'I didn't try to fool him.'

'Hell you didn't! And if I could have found those saddlebags you were so proud of, I—'

Then it had been Bishop who searched his quarters. And Colby would have been the rider in the hills who kept watch.

'You don't know what it's all about, Oran. Just shut up and listen,' Jordan snapped.

'You've got nothing to say I want to hear!'

'You'll hear it anyway—and I'm warning you all once more—make a wrong move and Crawford's a dead man. That clear?'

There was a long moment of silence and then Crawford said, 'Come on, come on, get it over with. What's on your mind?'

'Just this,' Ben said, 'I never stole that money.'

Crawford laughed, a low, forced chuckle. 'Don't give me that. I seen you, watched you ride off on that sorrel. All of us did, except Bishop there.'

'Wasn't me you saw. That horse and the jacket I'm wearing belonged to a man named

Woodward. Found him in a shack, dying.'

'And now you're tellin' me he handed over a pair of saddlebags loaded with twenty thousand dollars of the bank's money—'

'He did, but he didn't say it was hold-up money. Claimed he got it from selling some property—'

'And was on his way home when some outlaws, meanin' us, jumped him. That it?'

'Just what he said. He was shot up pretty bad. Made me promise to deliver the money to his wife here in Langford, personally. That's what I've been trying to do.'

'How's it happen you're forkin' his horse and wearin' his brush jacket?' Cleve Aaron asked, skeptically.

'Lost mine in a storm. Horse went over a cliff in the Mogollon Mountains with all I owned tied on the saddle. Was afoot when I ran into Woodward.'

Again there was silence. Oran Bishop spoke first. 'You expect us to swallow a yarn like that?'

Jordan swore impatiently. 'I don't give a damn what you think—it's the truth! And if I thought it was important enough I could take you back to where my buckskin is laying dead, half way down a canyon slope. I can show you where I buried Woodward. But it's not important.'

'What's important,' Crawford broke in, 'is the money. Where is it?'

'I haven't got it.'

'Haven't got it!' Gates echoed. 'What in the hell did you do—'

'Was on my way to hand it over to Woodward's widow, like I promised. Three men stopped me at the edge of town. They'd been watching for Woodward, and when they saw his horse, they figured something was wrong. Anyway they stopped me. One of them flashed a deputy marshal badge and said he was the law. He took the money, said he would turn it over to Mrs Woodward.'

'Did he?' Crawford asked in a low, tight voice.

'No—and he's not a lawman. Just found that out.'

'Not a deputy?' Crawford said, turning around slowly.

'He's an outlaw, same as the two men with him. They're together now. Woodward's widow is with them. They've got the money.'

Crawford's dark, intense face showed interest. 'Where?'

'Wait a minute, marshal,' Bishop said. 'You ain't falling for this yarn he's handing us, are you? It's ten to one he's cooking up a scheme to get you off his tail so's he can keep going with that money.'

'He sure don't have it on him now,' Crawford answered. 'And I reckon a man could get himself tangled into a mess, like he claims.'

'Only thing I'm interested in is clearing my name,' Jordan said. 'Give me your word there'll be no charges against me, and I'll help you nail the outlaws and get the bank's money back.'

At once Crawford said, 'Don't see why there'd be any reason to hold you, was you to do that. Far as I'm concerned, would prove you're tellin' the truth. Where is that bunch and the money?'

Jordan said, 'Then we've got a deal?'

'We have. Now where—'

'In that shack,' Ben said, handing Crawford his pistol. 'They're all there, even the woman.'

'For hell's sake,' Gates muttered in an amazed voice. 'That close?'

'How do you know?' Bishop demanded, still far from convinced.

'That's where I've been, listening to them talk. They figure to ride out after dark.'

'Only three of them, you said,' Cleve Aaron remarked. 'Won't be no trouble breakin' in and takin' over.'

'Wouldn't be easy,' Jordan said. 'Couple of us are bound to get killed. And, like I told you, Mrs Woodward's in there, too. Be smarter to wait until they come out. Not long now until dark.'

'Surround the place,' Gates suggested. 'Maybe they'd throw out their guns and quit.'

'Not them—not with twenty thousand dollars at stake. They'd fight and shootin' would bring half the town runnin' out here,' Crawford said, shaking his head. 'Never like outsiders hangin' around at a time like this. Always somebody gettin' shot accidental. I figure Jordan's got the best idea. We'll wait.'

CHAPTER SEVENTEEN

The others dismounted, led their horses into the dense brush and tied them. Crawford held back until they were again at his side.

'We'll move up, close as we can to the door,' he said. 'Best we spread out, cover it from all angles. Now, keep low. Don't want them spottin' us.'

They slipped off into the tangled growth, circling, to the east until they were directly opposite the cabin. They paused there briefly, then worked their way up to the edge of the tall weeds, rocks and scrubby bushes. No more than thirty feet of open yard now separated them from the doorway through which the outlaws would soon come.

Crawford, with whispers and gestures, placed his men at short intervals. Aaron was at the extreme left, then Arlie Davis, and Crawford. Next in the line was Oran Bishop, flanked by Jordan. Gates was at the right end.

'I'll give the word,' Crawford said, hunkering on his heels. 'Everybody wait for it.'

'I'm wonderin',' Gates murmured, 'is there a back door?'

Crawford glanced at Ben. 'How about it?'

Jordan shook his head, said, 'Only a small window. Could be a door around the side.'

'Take a look,' Crawford ordered, ducking his head at Gates. 'See where they got their horses, too.'

Gates made no answer but, on hands and knees, crawled off through the brush. He was back in only a few minutes.

'Ain't no door,' he said in a hushed voice. 'Just this one here in front. Three horses standin' in a corral behind the shack.'

'Supposed to be four,' Arlie Davis said.

'The woman walked here from her place,' Ben said. 'I followed her. She and Sharpe figure to ride double until they get a mount for her.'

'Somebody's comin' out,' Gates warned softly.

The door opened wide. Tubo Frick blocked the doorway. He glanced at the sky, judging the hour.

Crawford muttered, 'Frick—that lousy tinhorn—'

Jordan looked at the lawman. 'Know him?'

Crawford nodded. 'A long time. Probably

know the others, too. Same as I knew Woodward.'

Frick turned about, went into the cabin and closed the door. The low rumble of words coming from the dark interior of the shack ceased.

Ben felt Bishop's eyes upon him, twisted about to face the puncher. 'You convinced now I'm telling the truth? This proof enough?'

Bishop shrugged. 'Could be you figure you've got yourself in a jam. This would be a smart way out.'

Impatience sharpened Jordan's words. 'You don't make much sense! What would I get out of it? The bank will have its money back and I'll—'

'You'll save your own neck.'

Jordan spat in disgust. 'You're a plain fool, Oran. I wondered why Tom Ashburn didn't turn that job of ramroddin' over to you. Now I know.'

'Damn good thing for you I didn't find those saddlebags that night,' Bishop retorted. 'I'd have had you dead to rights then—could have proved to Ashburn what I suspected.'

'Or would you have grabbed them and run?' Ben suggested softly, deliberately baiting the man.

'Run—with the money? Why, damn you, I—'

'Forget it,' Bart Crawford snapped. 'You talk much louder and they'll be hearin' you.'

There was silence after that, broken only by the dry clack of insects, the chirping of birds in the trees, and the low cooing of doves. Over in the direction of Langford a dog was barking, and somewhere on a road to the north of the settlement, the drum of a hard running horse could be heard.

The minutes wore on, merged into an hour. As the sun lowered, tension mounted gradually within Ben Jordan. He could see the effects of the long wait putting its mark on Oran Bishop, also. But if it were being noted and felt by Crawford and his three men, there was no indication. They were old hands at it, he guessed. Likely this was far from the first such experience for them.

And it was not too different from certain days and nights in the *Barranca Negra*. There had been times when he, with his father and a few friends, had lain in wait for an expected raid by Mexican bandits. And later, after the death of his father, he had faced such danger without the reassuring presence of his parent.

But somehow it was different here. There were only strangers around him, men he did not know and therefore was unaware of their abilities—and reliability, if something went wrong. He wished now he could have some of those who had sided him during the black nights he sweated out in the Sonora desert: Felipe Alvarez—Jesus Calderon—Old Manuel—Cristobal Lopez, Mexicans all, he realized suddenly, yet he would have felt more at ease with them than the *gringos*—these men of his own race, crouched near him.

But there should be no trouble here. They were six to Sharpe's three, if you didn't count Ollie Woodward. Sharpe would recognize the futility of bucking such odds, and when called upon to throw down his guns, he would be smart enough to comply. And Frick and Rosen would follow his lead.

'Sun's gone,' Cleve Aaron said laconically. 'They ought to be comin' out.'

Crawford said, 'Be ready. Have your guns out. You know what to do when I give the word.'

'We're just waitin',' Aaron replied.

Ben Jordan fastened his eyes upon the closed door. He wished the outlaws would appear, surrender, and get the affair over with. He was beginning to feel the effect of the long hours, and the urge to get back to the Lazy A and assume his responsibilities was pushing him hard. There would be no trouble explaining it all to Tom Ashburn now. The rancher would listen, but if there were any doubts in his mind Bart Crawford could clear them up.

And that was the way Ben wanted it. No

doubts, no shadows. Tom Ashburn—and Sally, must believe in him and trust him, or else there was no future for him on the Lazy A. And they would, he was certain. Only Oran Bishop with his pig-headed stubbornness, might continue to doubt. While it meant little to him, he wished the blond puncher would see matters in their true light, and admit he was wrong. Oran was a man he'd like to call friend.

'Here they come...'

Gates' whisper was like a keen-bladed knife slicing through the half darkness. Ben stiffened as tension gripped him. There was a slight rustling sound as the men beside him prepared themselves.

'When I say the word—' Crawford murmured. 'Not before.'

Ollie Woodward came through the doorway, paused, glanced back into the cabin momentarily, and stepped out into the yard. She turned left, walked slowly toward the far side of the cabin.

Frick appeared next. Then Barney Rosen, carrying the near empty whiskey bottle by the neck. Both halted in front of the step. Al Sharpe loomed in the doorway. He swung the saddlebags over his shoulder and came on into the open. For a moment the three outlaws made a tight little group against the black rectangle of the cabin door.

Sharpe said, 'Let's get movin',' and started

to follow Ollie Woodward.

In the next fragment of time Bart Crawford rose to his feet. He said, 'No,' and instantly four guns opened up on the outlaws.

Sharpe, Frick and Rosen slammed back against the wall of the shack, dead from the hail of bullets. Through the boiling smoke and deafening echoes Ollie Woodward began to scream, a wild, piercing, unnerving sound that sliced to the bone.

Ben Jordan stood in horrified silence. Bishop, his mouth gaping, turned to Crawford slowly.

'My God—that was pure murder!' he said in a strangled voice. 'You never gave them a chance to—'

Crawford, calmly reloading his revolver, said, 'Didn't plan on it.' He glanced at Gates. 'Shut that woman up.'

Gates brought his gun up, leveled it. Crawford said, 'Not that way. Rap her over the head. That ought to do it.'

Arlie Davis and Cleve Aaron moved out of the brush, followed Gates. Ollie Woodward's screams faded before the men reached her. She pulled back against the side of the cabin, her eyes wide with terror as she stared down at the bullet riddled figures of the slain outlaws.

Jordan brushed aside the revolting sickness that had claimed him suddenly when hard suspicion had sprung to life. He took a half step toward Crawford. He watched the emotionless features of the man for several moments, and then he spoke.

'You're no different from them. You're killers, outlaws. You're not lawmen!'

Crawford finished reloading his weapon and brought it up abruptly, covering both Jordan and Bishop.

'You're smart, mister,' he said drily. 'Now drop your irons, right where you're standin'. Both of you. Then get over alongside the woman until I figure out what I ought to do.'

CHAPTER EIGHTEEN

Oran Bishop's question was a gasp. 'You—you're not lawmen?'

'Hell, no,' Crawford said. 'No more'n them three layin' there on the ground.'

'But you said—you told us—'

Crawford laughed. 'You think of a better way to go chasin' after a lot of stolen money? It's real easy, long as you ain't around where folks know you.' He motioned toward the shack with his gun. 'Move.'

Jordan gave Bishop a bitter, half smile. The blond puncher knew now how simple it was to get fooled. When a man told you he was a lawman and exhibited some simple proof, such as a badge, it never occurred to you to question him.

With Bishop, he walked out of the brush, crossed the small yard and lined up beside Ollie Woodward. Gates was hunched over Sharpe, pulling the saddlebags from beneath the dead outlaw's body. Davis and Cleve Aaron watched closely. Gates laid the pouches across Barney Rosen's back and freed the straps from their buckles.

'It's here,' he announced, thrusting his fingers inside and stirring about in the coins and currency.

Crawford said, 'Finally run it down. But we got to be thinkin' about driftin'. That shootin's goin' to bring half the town out here.'

Ollie Woodward, a forced smile on her face, moved toward Crawford. 'How about me?' she asked. 'Where do I come in? Was my husband who robbed that bank. I'm entitled to a share.'

'Like hell,' Crawford grunted. 'Was him that botched the deal up for us—him and them two owlhoots there with him. We were all set to clean out that bank ourselves. They beat us to it by about thirty minutes and got away with a stinkin' twenty thousand dollars. There was three times that much to be had! Woodward and his bunch didn't know that.'

Ollie smiled wider. 'Still a lot of money. Either you ought to give me a share, or else—'

'Or else what?' Crawford demanded.

Olivia Woodward tilted her head coyly. 'Or else take me along with you ... I can help you enjoy it.'

Arlie Davis said, quick and sudden, 'No, sir! We don't want no woman hangin' around!'

Crawford appraised the woman slowly. He grunted. 'Expect you could keep a man mighty busy, sure enough. And spend his money real fast, too, was you given the chance.'

'Then you'll take me?'

Crawford shook his head. 'Arlie's right. We got no room for a woman taggin' along. And there ain't much cash to split, anyway.'

'What are we doin' with these two jaspers?' Cleve Aaron asked, coming into the conversation. 'Not smart to leave them breathin' so's they can talk.'

'We won't,' Crawford said. 'We're goin' to make it look like a shoot-out between them and the others. But we got to move fast.'

Ollie flung a quick glance at Jordan and Bishop. She edged nearer to Crawford. 'You're not treating me right,' she said, protestingly—and threw herself directly into the outlaw leader's arms.

Crawford cursed, tried to step back, stumbled into Gates. In that moment Ben Jordan and Bishop, gambling everything against certain death, lunged forward.

Arlie Davis fired as Jordan swept Sharpe's pistol from its holster. Ben felt the outlaw's bullet burn along his neck. He triggered his weapon as he sprawled flat. Davis jolted as Jordan's slug caught him in the chest, drove him backwards.

Another gun blasted. Ben heard someone yell—Aaron he thought it was, but he did not turn to look but simply rolled. From the tail of his eye he saw Ollie Woodward still clinging to Bart Crawford. The outlaw was staggering about, struggling desperately to dislodge her. Ben saw Gates then, whirling to shoot. He dropped the man with a hasty shot.

Beyond him Oran Bishop was pulling himself to his feet. Blood was streaming down one arm which hung limply at his side. But the blond puncher was grinning, a tight lipped, hard cornered grin. Cleve Aaron lay motionless beneath him.

Jordan rolled to an upright position, leaped to where Ollie Woodward wrestled with Crawford. He seized the man's hand, wrenched the pistol from his grasp. The woman released her death-like grip and sank to the ground exhausted and breathless.

Crawford stared down at her, his dark face furious, eyes burning. 'A damned woman...' he muttered. 'Tricked by a damned woman.'

Jordan rubbed at the stinging groove along

his neck. 'You can think about that while they're hanging you for murder,' he said. He glanced at Bishop. 'Hit bad?'

Oran shook his head. 'Not much more than a scratch. You all right?'

'All I did get was a scratch. How about Aaron? He dead?'

'Knocked out. Couldn't get my hands on a gun. Had to use my fist.'

'That's two left for the law then,' Ben said, adding, 'the real law this time.'

He reached down for Ollie Woodward's hand, helped her rise. She was breathing more normally now, and womanlike, she began to pin up her hair, shaken loose by Crawford's frantic attempts to break away from her.

'No need for you to wait here,' he said. 'Take my horse—your husband's—and go back to your house before anybody gets here. The town won't ever know you had any part of this.'

Ben glanced at Bishop, standing with a gun pressed into Crawford's back. The blond puncher nodded his approval.

Ollie Woodward gave him a grateful smile. 'Thank you,' she murmured.

'We sure owe you that much,' Bishop said.

Off, somewhere along the lane, the beat of oncoming horses sounded.

'You'd better hurry,' Jordan said. 'You'll find that sorrel over there in the brush. Keep off the road. You won't be noticed.'

She nodded, ran across the yard. At the fringe of the brush she paused, looked back. 'He's still your horse,' she said. 'When you get ready to leave he'll be waiting for you—with a bill of sale.'

She was gone in the next moment, out of sight in the weeds and brush. Jordan turned and pulled off his belt. Jerking Crawford about, he strapped the outlaw's wrists together. With Bishop helping, they did the same for Cleve Aaron, using a strip of rawhide they found on Barney Rosen's body. They put both men inside the cabin and waited outside the doorway for the riders they could hear coming.

Bishop stuck out his hand. 'Reckon I sure made a real prime jackass out of myself,' he said. 'That Crawford sure fooled me.'

'We both weren't very bright,' Ben agreed.

Bishop was quiet. Inside the shack Crawford was cursing in a low, furious tone. Aaron, conscious and sitting up, was looking around in a dazed, puzzled way.

Oran Bishop studied the toes of his boots. 'Know I don't have much right to say this, but I hope what you said about me staying on the ranch still goes.'

Jordan shrugged. 'All right with me. Up to you to square yourself with Tom Ashburn though.'

'Won't be no chore. Crawford took him

in, same as he did me. But I figure I'd better warn you. Still think I'm the best man for that ramrod job and I aim to keep on working for it. If you don't favor that, you'd better fire me now.'

'I'm not afraid of holding it.'

'Good enough. Just so you know. And there's one thing more—Sally.'

'What about Sally?'

'I figure to keep trying there, too.'

Jordan grinned. 'You just do that, cowboy. She'll pick the best man—just like her pa did.'